TRIPLE FAULT

Other books in the
CANTERWOOD CREST SERIES:

TAKE THE REINS

CHASING BLUE

BEHIND THE BIT

CANTERWOOD
CREST

TRIPLE FAULT

JESSICA BURKHART

ALADDIN MIX
New York London Toronto Sydney

This book is a work of fiction. Any references to historical events, real people, or real locales are used fictitiously. Other names, characters, places, and incidents are the product of the author's imagination, and any resemblance to actual events or locales or persons, living or dead, is entirely coincidental.

m!x

ALADDIN M!X

Simon & Schuster Children's Publishing Division

1230 Avenue of the Americas, New York, NY 10020

First Aladdin M!X edition August 2009

Text copyright © 2009 by Jessica Burkhart

All rights reserved, including the right of reproduction
in whole or in part in any form.

ALADDIN is a trademark of Simon & Schuster, Inc., and related logo
is a registered trademark of Simon & Schuster, Inc.

ALADDIN M!X and related logo are registered trademarks
of Simon & Schuster, Inc.

For information about special discounts for bulk purchases, please
contact Simon & Schuster Special Sales at 1-866-506-1949
or business@simonandschuster.com.

The Simon & Schuster Speakers Bureau can bring authors to your live event.
For more information or to book an event contact the Simon & Schuster Speakers
Bureau at 1-866-248-3049 or visit our website at www.simonspeakers.com.

Designed by Jessica Handelman

The text of this book was set in Venetian 301 BT.

Manufactured in the United States of America

10

Library of Congress Control Number 2009924911

ISBN 978-1-4169-5843-7

ISBN 978-1-4169-9637-8 (eBook)

0414 OFF

To Kate Angelella.
For pink and purple edits.
For encouraging the sparkly.
For Brooklyn.

ACKNOWLEDGMENTS

Alyssa Henkin, the plaque for Best Agent will be arriving at your office any day now.

Kate Angelella, just try to make this process more fun, okay? Seriously.

Thanks to everyone at S&S—especially Jessica "the Other Jess" Handelman, Nicole Russo, Lucille Rettino, and Venessa Williams.

Monica Stevenson, this is the most gorgeous cover photo. Thank you, Canterwood models!

Lesley Ward and Allison Griest at *Young Rider*, thanks for supporting Canterwood.

Thanks to my family and friends for all of their support.

Finally, hugs to all of the fans who have sent me e-mails, notes, and photos. You're the best and you make me feel like a rock star.

TRIPLE FAULT

I

SWAK,
ALMOST,

JUST SAY IT, I TOLD MYSELF. ANSWER HIM.
I shifted on the tack trunk outside Charm's stall. You're supposed to reply when someone asks if they can kiss you. But with Eric just inches from my face, staring at me expectantly, I could barely think, let alone formulate a whole sentence.

My horse, Charm, snorted as he looked down at us like he too was waiting to hear my answer. And the truth was, right now I wasn't thinking about how my ex–best friend Callie and my almost-boyfriend Jacob had betrayed me. Or how I'd almost blown my chance in front of the Youth Equestrian National Team scouts. I knew for sure what my answer was—I wanted to kiss Eric.

And by the ecstatic look on his face, it was clear that he knew what I was thinking.

His black hair fell over one eye as he leaned closer to me. I ignored the whooshing sound in my ears and the nerves making my stomach swirl. Eric's lips were about to touch mine. My eyes fluttered shut.

Oh.

My.

"Eric?" someone called.

Our heads jerked up.

"Eric?" the man's voice called again.

Mr. Conner! Our riding instructor's boots thudded down the aisle.

"Omigod!" I whispered, jumping up off the tack trunk. I stumbled sideways and Eric stood up to grab me—keeping me upright. I tried to will the flush out of my cheeks.

"Just be cool," Eric whispered, laughing.

"Gee, thanks!" I hissed, my cheeks still hot.

Mr. Conner walked up to us. He stopped and his dark eyes zeroed in on *me*!

"Wewerejusttalkingaboutthedemo," I rambled.

Eric shot me an it's-cute-when-you-dork-out look and I mushed my lips closed.

"Okay," Mr. Conner said, staring at me for a second.

I squirmed. Did I have an I-almost-kissed-a-boy look on my face?

I draped one arm over Charm's stall door and leaned against it, trying to look casual.

"Eric, I need your help finding some paperwork for the scouts before they leave," Mr. Conner said.

"Sure," Eric agreed.

"See you around," I said to Eric. "Or not. I mean, I'm not going to look for you or anything. You know. If I see you—great. If not, that's fine too."

Stop talking! I yelled to myself.

Mr. Conner looked at me again, shaking his head slightly, before walking back down the aisle.

Eric began to follow him, but then turned back to look at me. "Very cool," he mouthed.

I rolled my eyes, but I couldn't help grinning. When Mr. Conner and Eric were gone, I slumped against Charm's stall door. Life as a famous actress was not in my future.

"Hey," Paige Parker, my friend and roommate, said as she walked up to me. "Ready to go back to the room?"

Earlier in the afternoon, Paige had come to the stable to watch me ride in the demonstration for the YENT

scouts, but she had no idea how much drama had gone down behind the scenes.

"I'll meet you there," I said. "I just need a few minutes with Charm." *And to wait for Eric.*

Paige nodded. "Okay." She paused, almost like she suspected something was wrong, but I gave her a bright smile before she left.

I slipped into Charm's stall and hugged his neck. He blinked sleepily as I rubbed his blaze and reached up to straighten his chestnut mane. I almost had to stand on my tiptoes to reach up by his ears. Even for a Thoroughbred/Belgian mix, he was tall.

"I almost kissed Eric!" I whispered giddily to Charm. Not even the awful things that had happened today could erase my *this-close*-to-kissing excitement.

"Look," I told Charm, "I know our ride got messed up because I was upset about Jacob, but the scouts said that they thought I was just nervous—so that's good."

There were still up to three open YENT seats for the five of us on the Canterwood advanced team. If Charm and I wowed the scouts at the upcoming June tryouts, we had a chance. If not, our YENT dreams were over.

Buzz.

I flipped open my phone. It was Eric.

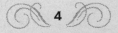

Stuck w Mr. C for an hr or more. Sry. Txt u ltr?

Sigh. *No prob. TTYL.*

I wanted to see Eric *now*. But wait. Then we might actually . . . kiss. And now that I'd had time to think about it, I was starting to wonder if I was prepared enough. I had no clue how to kiss a boy—what if I was horrible? Now I was glad Mr. Conner had interrupted us. I needed kissing tips stat.

I gave Charm a final pat. "Bye, boy."

As I headed for the exit, horses and riders began trickling into the aisle from the arena. Visiting students had armfuls of blankets, tail wraps, and leg bandages to prepare their horses for the trip home. I ducked my head, suddenly wishing I was invisible—there were too many people I didn't want to run into. But as I skirted around a blue roan mare in crossties, I turned a sharp corner and almost slammed right into Callie and Jacob.

I held back a groan. Jacob's eyes flicked from me to the ground.

"Sasha, please," Callie said. Her voice sounded wobbly and her pink eyes told me that she'd definitely been crying. "Can't we just—"

I turned away. "I have to go," I said.

"Sash," Jacob pleaded. His gray-green eyes finally

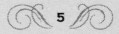

connected with mine. He really did look sorry, but I didn't care.

It killed me to see them standing next to each other—so familiar and easy. The worst part was that they had been going behind my back this whole time. Callie had even been mad at me because she thought I'd been interested in Eric. Which, at the time, I wasn't. At the time, all I could think about was Jacob. And I guess all Jacob was thinking about was Callie.

I shook my head and, sidestepping Callie, walked out the door. I shivered in the chilly March air and wrapped my arms across my chest. The campus was eerily quiet. Most of the Canterwood students wouldn't be back from midwinter break until tomorrow. The sun, which had been bright during testing, had slipped behind a fat gray cloud. I kicked a patch of dry brown grass with my boot. I didn't know how to feel. One second I was giddy from my almost kiss with Eric. And the next I wanted to curl up in a ball because of what Callie and Jacob had done.

For the first time in a while, I wished I were home. Mom would bring me raspberry tea in bed and Dad would sing embarrassing old-people songs and play air guitar to make me laugh. But now it was too late to go home—classes started on Monday.

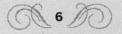

I didn't want to think about sitting through English class with Callie. Some best friend. If only I had a class with Eric instead. Just thinking about him made me smile. I'd been all about Jacob for months—so much that I'd missed noticing what a cute, smart, and amazing guy Eric was. Until today, I'd only thought of Jacob in that way. Ugh. Did not want to think about Jacob.

I yanked open the door of Winchester Hall and stepped into the warm hallway. The cheery yellow walls didn't make me feel any better. I just wanted to hide in my room.

Trudging past the common room, I stopped when a girl's voice pierced the stillness of the hallway.

"Do NOT drag my Coach luggage! And hurry up. I'd like to be moved in before the semester is over."

Ohhhhh, no.

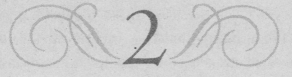

UN-WELCOME TO
WINCHESTER

I BURIED MY FACE IN MY HANDS.

"Don't tip my trunk!" the girl snapped.

Without even looking, I knew the voice—and the trunk—belonged to Jasmine King, the former Wellington Prep seventh grader who'd just transferred to Canterwood. Jas was so awful that she made Heather Fox, Canterwood Queen Bee and my archenemy, look sweet. And that was NOT easy. Heather's weapons of choice were intimidation and threats. Jasmine was all action.

"Omigod, could you guys, like, move any slower?" Jasmine asked the movers.

I'd thought this day couldn't get any more dramatic.

So. Wrong.

Jasmine moving into Winchester might have been the

worst thing ever—which, considering the fact that I'd just found out that my ex-BFF and ex-BF were dating, was really saying something.

I dragged myself down the hallway and around the corner. Oh, my God. It was an explosion of luggage. Crocodile-skin bags, rolling suitcases, duffels, satchels, and other luggage that I didn't even know what to call had been stacked from floor to ceiling. Two muscley guys lifted one of the massive trunks, their faces reddening as they carried it through the doorway.

"Sasha!" Jasmine said, grinning at me. "You came to welcome me to Winchester!"

"Um, not really," I said.

Jas pouted. "Why not?"

"Oh, I don't know. How about because you tried to intimidate my team at regionals, you poured oil on Aristocrat before Heather's class, and you 'accidentally' spilled molasses on my head at the clinic." I folded my arms.

Jasmine waved a manicured hand at me. "Oh, please. We'll have fun! And look!" She pointed to a luggage-filled room. "I'm only two doors away from you."

"Super," I muttered. I watched as the guys continued to lug suitcases inside. Jasmine stood with her hands on her hips, the look on her face daring them to drop her luggage.

"Hello!" she barked at one of the movers when he almost lost his grip on the trunk. "Be careful with that!"

"That room was empty before," I said. "Who's your roommate?"

Jasmine shook her head. "Livvie said I could have the room all to myself 'cause I'm starting the semester late. I just explained that it would help me adjust better if I had my own room to retreat to. Besides, who needs a roommate when you've got teammates?"

I tried not to roll my eyes. Livvie, the Winchester dorm monitor, had to have seen right through Jas's fake-angel act. Didn't she?

"Yeeeaaah," I said. "Whatever. I need to get to my room."

I hopped over a duffel bag and squeezed along the wall, trying not to cause a luggage avalanche.

Jasmine sighed. "This place isn't *anything* like Wellington's dorms, but I'll make it work."

If she hated Canterwood this much, why didn't she go back to her old school already?

"I think it's nice," I said.

"You *would*."

I rolled my eyes but didn't respond. It just wasn't worth it.

"I can't wait to meet everyone else," Jasmine said. She pulled out a lip gloss—a vanilla-cherry flavor I did *not* have—and smoothed it on. "We can have movie nights in the common room!"

I stared at her. Kidding, right? *"We* might, but *you* won't. Unless you start being nicer, no one's going to hang out with you."

I walked away from Jasmine and her posse of movers. I pulled open my door, relieved to get away from her and everyone else.

"Can you *believe* this?" I wailed to Paige the second the door slammed behind me.

"What?" Paige asked, swiveling in her desk chair to look at me.

"Jasmine is moving into Winchester!"

"Jasmine King? Are you serious? That's who that was?"

I realized I'd told Paige all about Jasmine and her nastiness, but she'd never met her before.

"Yes! It wasn't enough that she tried to make my team lose at the Junior Equestrian Regionals *or* that she made me miserable during Mr. Conner's clinic. Now she lives here too."

Paige shook her head. "I can't believe she got assigned to Winchester."

"She even got her own room. Two. Doors. Away."

"That's not fair." Paige frowned. "But I guess it's hard to switch schools in the middle of the semester. Livvie probably thought it would be stressful for Jas to move in with a girl she'd never talked to before. Even you and I got to e-mail over the summer before school started so we could get to know each other, remember?"

I kicked off my boots and rummaged through my closet for clean clothes. "No way Jas would ever worry about a roommate. Trust me."

Paige shrugged. "Maybe not." She looked as if she wanted to say something else, but stopped.

I knew Paige thought I was just angry about Jasmine— she didn't know what had happened with Callie and Jacob. But I wasn't quite ready to talk about it yet—I could barely even think about it.

I shook my head, pulling a change of clothes out of my closet. One thing was for sure—Winchester was never going to be the same.

3

POISONED HOT
CHOCOLATE, YUM!

I ROLLED OVER AND SQUINTED AT MY ALARM
clock. 4:37 in the morning. I snuggled under my comforter and tried to go back to sleep, but it was no use. My brain wouldn't let me sleep. Scenes from yesterday played over and over in my head—Jacob watching Callie ride, Callie realizing that I knew the truth, Eric almost kissing me.

I tried to think about something—anything—else. If I could just focus on riding. But it would still be a week and a half before I could ride again. Mr. Conner had banned me along with the rest of the advanced team.

Violet, Brianna, and Georgia—three eighth graders who called themselves the Belles—were banned too. It happened after the Belles dared us to ride our horses across campus at night just so we could join their exclusive little clique. They had been pressuring us to do the dare when Mr. Conner showed up—but he didn't come in time to prevent me from seeing a new side to Callie. She, Julia, and Alison had agreed to do the Belles' dare. Heather and I had refused for the safety of our horses.

Now I stared up at the dark ceiling. *Think of something happy*, I told my brain. Eric. I smiled. He'd only transferred to Canterwood in January, but he'd already become such a big part of my life. Initially, we bonded over our mutual love of horses. But I recently found out that it had been more than that for Eric. He'd known that I was with Jacob, though, so he never even let on that he liked me as more than a friend.

The more I thought about Eric, the more I realized how important he was to me. I decided right then—at, ugh, 4:59 a.m.—that my relationship with him was *not* going to be like what I'd had with Jacob. No one could know Eric and I were together just yet. If the Trio—Heather and her BFFs, Julia and Alison—found out, they'd probably, no, *definitely*, try to break us up. Just like they tried to do with Jacob, before Callie single-handedly took care of that for them.

This time no one would have a chance to mess up

whatever I was starting with Eric. I couldn't let Heather, Callie, or anyone else ruin it. Eric and I needed time to figure things out. And to . . . kiss. I smiled. Kissing was definitely a happy thing to focus on.

Tap! Tap!

"Paige?" I mumbled, groggy with sleep.

"No," she said. "I think someone's at the door." She slid out of bed.

"It's seven fifteen on a Sunday. Who could that be?"

I covered my face with my pillow as Paige opened the door.

"Morning!"

I whipped my pillow off my face and sat up. It was Jasmine, holding a cardboard tray with three cups of something from the Sweet Shoppe and smiling.

"Omigod," Jas said, staring at Paige. "You're *the* Paige Parker from the *Teen Cuisine* website. I'm, like, the biggest fan of the show! I can't wait till your episodes air."

"Thanks," Paige replied with a polite smile. She couldn't be rude to anyone—it wasn't in her DNA. Paige glanced at me. I smoothed down my bed-head fly-aways and tried to ignore the fact that Jasmine's outfit was totally perfect. Black skinny jeans tucked into tall caramel brown boots with an oversize, belted baby blue sweater.

"I'm Jasmine." She gave her best I'm-so-innocent smile. "I just moved into Winchester. I wanted to introduce myself. I brought you guys hot chocolate."

She held out the tray with flourish. Paige, hesitating for a second, took a cup.

"Thank you," Paige said. "And, um, let us know if you need help finding something on campus."

Jasmine gave a tiny smile. "I sooo will."

Paige raised the cup to her lips.

"Don't!" I yelled. I tossed back my covers and ran over to Paige, not caring that I was still in my pink pajamas dotted with silver hearts.

I grabbed the cup from Paige and set it on her desk.

"What's wrong?" Paige asked at the same time that Jas said, "Omigod, what are you *doing*?"

"Don't even think about drinking that," I told Paige. "She probably spit in it. Or poisoned it somehow."

"Sasha," Jas said. She fake sniffed and took a step back. "I was just trying to be a good neighbor." She shrugged and, I swear, her eyes started to tear up. "See you," she said to Paige.

"Nice to meet you," Paige said.

I shut the door and locked it. And double-checked the lock.

Paige nodded at the hot chocolate. "You really think she did something to it?"

"For sure."

Paige seemed to consider this. "But she seemed upset. For real. Maybe Jasmine knows she has to change. She's not visiting Canterwood anymore. She's living here. She can't be mean to everyone or she'll never make any friends."

"Maybe," I said. "But I still don't trust her."

An hour later my phone beeped and I looked at the screen. *Want 2 meet @ stable?*

Eric! I ignored the seven missed calls from Callie and texted back. *Sure. C u in 10.*

"I'm going to skip breakfast," I announced.

"Meeting Callie?" Paige asked.

I shook my head. "Not exactly. Some . . . stuff happened yesterday. I've got to go, but I'll tell you about it when I get back."

"Something happened?" Paige questioned. "Like what? Sasha?"

"Just . . ." I paused. I couldn't even get the words out. "I'll tell you later, okay?"

Paige's eyes stayed on my face for a second, but she must have been able to tell I *really* didn't want to talk about it then, because she said, "You can't ignore my questions forever, Sasha Silver. You've got to tell me everything when you get back."

"I will," I promised.

Paige gave me The Eye.

"I swear!" I said, cracking a smile.

Once Paige left for breakfast, I tugged off the grass-stained breeches I'd planned to wear and pulled on my new chocolate-colored pair. Oh. Not as if I needed to wear breeches—I couldn't ride. But it was habit. Shrugging, I left them on and went into the bathroom.

I'm going to see Eric! I'm going to see Eric! I sang in my head.

This called for something beyond my normal makeup routine. I smoothed on tinted moisturizer, darkened my lashes with brown mascara—twice—and carefully applied pale pink gloss. After brushing my hair, putting it up, and taking it back down again, I went back to my room and put on my boots and coat.

One more mirror check. I peeked at my reflection, then took a breath. *It's just Eric,* I reminded myself as

I left the room. My pace slowed as I walked down the hallway. But I wasn't going to see Eric my *friend*. Eric was . . . what? Not my boyfriend. Not yet. But I'd never even *almost* kissed a boy before. What if I was the worst kisser *ever*?! Eric could kiss me, hate it, and never talk to me again. I could do everything wrong and totally embarrass myself.

Yesterday, the almost kiss had happened so fast, there had been no time to freak out. Well, there was plenty of time to panic now! I could *not* repulse Eric with my lack of lip-lock skills.

For a second, I considered going back to Winchester. But I kept going. I could do this.

I walked across the stable yard and saw Eric standing by the outdoor round pen. Troy, one of the seventh-grade intermediate riders, trotted his horse in small circles. I wasn't sure if I was relieved or disappointed to see him. Eric definitely wouldn't kiss me for the first time in front of Troy.

I couldn't hide my smile as I walked over to Eric. No matter what kind of mood I was in, Eric always made me happy.

"Hey," I said, trying not to wobble as I walked.

Eric flashed a smile that made my nerves disappear.

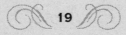

"Hi," he said, digging his hands into the pockets of his gray wool pullover.

"They look good," I said, nodding at Troy and his horse.

"Troy's been schooling Gavin for almost an hour," Eric said. "Gavin was stiff when they started, but look at the way he's flexing his neck now."

I stepped closer to the fence to see. Gavin, moving at a relaxed trot, paid attention to Troy's every signal.

"He's got it now," I said.

We watched for a few more minutes. The sun warmed my face and I forgot that it was actually cold outside.

"Want to go into the stable?" Eric asked.

"Sure." I half wanted to ask Troy if he'd like to come.

"See you around," Eric called to Troy.

"See ya," Troy said, barely looking up as he asked Gavin for a working trot.

Eric and I started across the yard to the stable. The dark lacquered barn was my favorite place on campus. It was immaculate—inside and out—and warm, and it wasn't one of those stables where riders were afraid to drop a stalk of hay on the floor. If we did, Mr. Conner just expected us to pick it up.

"How're you feeling about . . . things?" Eric asked.

"Well," I told him, "I'm frustrated that I almost blew my chance at the YENT because I was upset about Jacob and Callie. I can't let that happen again."

Eric nodded. "You'll be ready next time, I know it."

His arm brushed mine, and my skin tingled even through my winter coat! I tried not to make the OMG-Eric-touched-me face. But I was five seconds away from going into full-out giggly girl mode.

"What do you want to do?" I asked.

"Since you, uh, can't ride, I figured we could groom Charm and Luna," Eric said. "I mean, if you want."

"Sure, but don't you want to ride?"

"Nah, that's cool," Eric said. "I kind of just wanted to hang out with *you*."

I shook my head. "No, it's totally fine. And I could coach you, if you want."

"Really?" Eric asked.

"Go tack up and I'll meet you in the indoor arena."

"Give me five minutes," Eric said.

We split up and I took a side aisle into the empty indoor arena. I kicked my toe in the dirt. Being stuck on the ground was the worst! Charm and I should have been soaring over jumps right now. I sighed. For now I could concentrate on helping Eric. And if I focused on him,

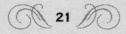

I wouldn't think about riding Charm. Or kissing.

"Ready, Coach Silver?" Eric called in a teasing voice. He led Luna, the stable horse he often rode, over to me.

"Mr. Rodriguez," I said, mimicking Mr. Conner's deep voice. "Let's get started."

4

FAN GIRL

ERIC LOOKED EVEN CUTER ON HORSEBACK. He guided Luna to the arena's edge and turned to me, waiting for instructions. When I looked at him, I forgot all about Callie and Jacob.

"Walk, please," I said.

Luna started forward and Eric sat tall in the saddle. He and Luna made a couple of large circles around me. Luna, a flea-bitten gray mare, was perfect for Eric. She listened to him, but she could be fiery too.

"Posting trot," I called out.

Eric rose in the saddle but posted on the wrong lead. I opened my mouth, then closed it. I *had* been about to tell him he was on the wrong lead. But what if I hurt his feelings? I'd offered to coach him, but I hadn't thought about how weird it would feel to point out what he was doing wrong.

"Um, Eric," I started. "I think you're on the wrong lead."

Eric looked down at Luna's shoulder. "You're right." He sat for a beat before posting on the right lead.

He circled me three times. I chewed on my cheek, wanting to give him pointers, but I couldn't. After a few minutes, Eric asked Luna to walk. He rode into the arena's center and stopped in front of me. He pushed his helmet back and looked down at me.

"Sash, you do know that I *want* your help, right? I can tell you're holding back. Tell me what you really think. C'mon. Channel Mr. Conner."

I blinked up at him. "You sure?"

"I think I can take it." He smiled.

Just go for it, I told myself. "Fine. You asked for it." I put my hands on my hips. "Circle once at a sitting trot and then canter."

"Better!" Eric said. Luna trotted for a few seconds before Eric urged her into a canter.

Eric's legs were still, but his hands inched into the air.

"Lower your hands," I called. Eric dropped his hands and I smiled to myself. I could do this.

"Sitting trot, bring her through the center, and change directions," I said.

Eric brought Luna to a smooth trot. I watched his legs, hands, and back. All fine. But after a few seconds, my attention started to wander. I visualized us on the trails, riding side by side. It would start to snow, and Eric would have flakes stuck to his eyelashes. We'd stop by the creek and he'd brush the snow out of my hair. Then he'd lean in and . . .

"Sasha?"

I jumped. "Huh? What?" I asked.

"Are my hands okay?" Eric asked.

"Yes, yep," I stammered. I shook my head, covering my smile with my hand. I had to pay attention. I wanted Eric to be the best on the intermediate team. If only Eric had transferred to Canterwood in time for the advanced team tryouts. But he'd make it this fall.

Half an hour later, Luna's coat started to darken with sweat. I'd somehow managed to focus for the rest of the lesson and hadn't let up on Eric once. I *might* have taken out some of my frustration about Callie and Jacob on Eric. I'd been making him work hard.

"Pull her up for a sec," I said. "Then you can jump."

Eric stopped Luna in front of me and wiped fake sweat

off his forehead. "For a second, I thought you were going to make me do a sitting trot until my legs fell off!"

"I considered it," I teased. "But I felt sorry for Luna."

Eric laughed. "Weren't you afraid to critique me, what, half an hour ago?"

"I guess I got over that!"

"You think?"

The dizzy/warm feeling swept through me. I pretended to be fascinated by Luna's bridle so I didn't have to look at Eric.

"What's my jumping order, coach?" Eric asked.

I looked at the far side of the arena. "The two verticals, the oxer, the double oxer, another vertical, turn, and then take the jump with the flower boxes."

"Okay. I'll try not to embarrass myself," Eric said.

"Oh, please," I said. "You'll be fine. Count strides in your head if you need to."

Eric nodded, touching his crop to his helmet in a salute. "Here goes!"

I crossed my fingers as he urged Luna into a canter and pointed her toward the first red and white vertical. *Please don't knock a rail*, I thought. I didn't want Eric to feel self-conscious if he messed up in front of me.

Luna tucked her forelegs under her body as she leaped

into the air. She landed with ease on the other side and started toward the next vertical. She jumped it and headed for the oxer—white boards with caution cones on either side. Mr. Conner wanted to introduce our horses to as many strange objects as possible. That would help cut down on spooks during show jumping or cross-country. Luna's ears flicked back when she saw the cones, but Eric deepened his seat and squeezed his legs against her sides. Luna jumped without hesitation.

As Eric guided Luna over the other obstacles and headed to the final jump, I didn't want to blink and miss a second of his ride. Eric must be one of the best show jumpers at Canterwood! His timing was *insane*, and he encouraged Luna to be confident as she jumped.

Eric slowed Luna to a trot and patted her neck. She tossed her head, sending her mane flying.

"I can't believe you!" I said. I hurried over to Luna and tried not to jump up and down like a fan girl at a rock concert. "You *never* told me you could jump like that."

Eric smiled as he dismounted. "Is that good or bad?"

"Oh, stop," I whacked his arm. "That was amazing, Eric. Seriously. You're one of the best jumpers at school and you know it."

He laughed. "I don't know about that, but thanks.

That means a lot coming from the cross-country star."

Luna snorted and I rubbed her shoulder. She'd been amazing too.

Eric took off his helmet and snapped it to one of the stirrup irons. "It's only because I have the most talented, awesome instructor. And cute. I mean, that Mr. Conner is so . . ."

Eric burst into laughter when he got a look at my face. "Kidding! I'm talking about *you*, Coach Silver."

"Oh," I whispered, feeling a blush burning my cheeks.

Luna, probably bored with our talking, nudged Eric's arm.

"I'll walk with you while you cool her out," I said.

"Okay. And feel free to critique me," Eric said.

I mock-rolled my eyes. "Yeah, after that jumping round, you *really* need help. No way you won't make the advanced team in the fall."

I helped Eric untack Luna, and after he left the stable, I spent a few minutes with Charm, who was in desperate need of a treat. A couple of days ago, I'd managed to sneak a bit of cake frosting into the stable fridge as a surprise for Charm. I brought him a carrot coated with vanilla frosting.

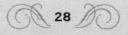

I laughed as he devoured the carrot, icing sticking to his whiskers. "Aw, Charm," I said. "Let me get a paper towel."

I walked to the tack room and paused when I heard voices inside.

"Oh, my gosh. He is *the* hottest guy at the stable," said a girl.

"Yeah, Rachel, but so is Ben," said another voice.

I peered through the slightly open door and saw six of the beginner and intermediate riders huddled together in the tack room. Who were they talking about? I grinned—Callie would absolutely love this. It was perfect gossip. I reached for my phone and stopped. Oh. For a second, I'd almost forgotten I couldn't call her.

"So is Andy!" added another girl. "I heart him. But Eric's definitely the hottest."

No.

Way.

They were talking about Eric! I peered through the door and watched the girls toss a purple rubber curry-comb around.

"That hair," said one of the beginners. "And his smile. He actually said hi to me yesterday. I thought I was going to die."

The girl sighed. Over Eric. My Eric.

I shook my head. These girls—all of them—noticed how amazing (and adorable) Eric was. How had I missed it for so long?

"He doesn't have a girlfriend," one girl said. "I'm sure of it. I bet he asks me out!"

Okaaay. This was getting to be a little much for me. Jealously flared in my chest. I knew Eric wasn't interested in anyone else, but still. I didn't even want to think about him going out with another girl. *I* hadn't even been out with him yet!

"He could ask *me* out," said a girl holding a Sprite.

"No, he already said hi to me, remember? Next step— a date."

This was torture! I held myself back from walking inside and shouting, "He's mine! Taken!"

I couldn't say that. Instead, I just stepped into the tack room without saying a word. The girls looked up at me.

"Hey," they said.

"Hi," I said, taking my time getting a paper towel.

"Well, when Eric asks me out first," said a girl with braces, "I won't say, 'Told you so.'"

I turned, pretending to look surprised. "Are you talking about Eric Rodriguez?"

The girls nodded, their heads doing the bobblehead thing.

"He's got a girlfriend," I said. "I heard it from one of my friends in Winchester."

Their gleeful expressions faded. "Seriously?" said one of the intermediate riders.

"Sorry," I said. "I hear they're superclose." I started toward the door, trying to keep myself from smiling.

"So, Eric's taken," a girl said. There were a few seconds of silence. "What about Troy?"

I held back my laughter until I was safely down the hallway.

When I got back to Winchester, Paige was waiting for me. She pointed to my desk chair. "Sit," she commanded.

I sat, surprised.

"What exactly happened at the end of the clinic?" Paige asked. "You haven't talked to Callie all day and you're not even trying to talk to Jacob."

I knew I owed Paige an explanation.

"Jacob and I are never getting back together," I said, wanting to get this part over with fast. "He came to the clinic to see Callie. They started talking after the Sweetheart Soirée and now they're going out."

Paige sat up straighter at the end of her bed. "Are you serious? Sasha, I'm so sorry. And Callie just told you on Saturday?"

"Nope. Julia did. Callie said she never meant for it to happen and she really, really likes Jacob . . ." I sighed. "I *just* got her back as my friend after the Eric mess."

"She ignored you for weeks because she thought you liked Eric, even though you didn't, and now—"

"And now I find out she was keeping the Jacob thing from me all this time," I finished.

"I can't believe her," Paige said. "It's hard to imagine Callie doing something like that."

"I know." I got up and walked over to my closet, busying myself by searching for an outfit for school tomorrow. "I never thought she'd go behind my back like that."

"At least Jacob never got that e-mail you sent him during the clinic," Paige said.

I nodded. "That would have been embarrassing. He would have gotten my 'Hey, Jacob. I still like you and want you back' e-mail after he was already with Callie. Awkward."

"You don't think the Belles will try to use the e-mail against you again, do you?" Paige asked.

I bit my lip. I still hadn't been able to figure out how

the Belles had found out about my confessional e-mail to Jacob. They'd used their knowledge of the e-mail to black-mail me into almost participating in the stupid dare that got me suspended from riding. The only explanation I'd been able to come up with was that they somehow hacked into my e-mail. Thankfully, Jacob said he'd never gotten the e-mail . . . and with any luck, it was sitting in some spam-mail folder somewhere, never to be seen again.

"I don't know," I confessed to Paige. "But it doesn't matter—Jacob's with Callie now."

I considered telling Paige about Eric, but something stopped me. I wanted to keep the secret to myself for just a little while longer.

5

BIOHAZARD

"I CAN'T BELIEVE IT'S ALREADY MONDAY morning!" Paige called from the bathroom. She put her brush away and stepped out, looking fab in dark-wash jeans with brown patent leather ankle boots and a blue and white striped sweater. She looked like she'd stepped off the set of *Teen Cuisine*—the soon-to-be-aired cooking show she hosted. Paige would so be dressing me when I got ready for my future first date with Eric.

"Don't remind me," I said. I opened up my e-mail and clicked on a message from Mr. Conner.

Dear seventh and eighth grade advanced teams:
Even though you are not allowed to ride,

it's expected that you will care for your horses
in the morning until your lessons resume.

—Mr. Conner

Not that I'd ever skip seeing Charm in the morning anyway—but the Trio was probably groaning about still having to get up superearly to groom their horses.

"I've got to go," Paige said, grabbing her messenger bag and piling her arms with books. "I have to meet with my English teacher before class. See you at lunch!"

She left and I pulled on a pair of jeans, a red waffle-knit shirt, and my paddock boots. As I left Winchester and headed across campus, I realized that my chances of avoiding Callie were basically zero. She'd be at the stable caring for Black Jack, her supersweet Morab gelding.

I figured Callie might try to apologize again, but I still wasn't ready to hear it. Callie had texted and called me half a dozen times, but I'd deleted the unopened texts and let the voice mails pile up in my inbox. The back-and-forth of being friends one minute and not the next was too painful. And now Jacob was involved. I didn't even want to think about what I'd say to him when film class started. Ugh.

When I passed Jack's stall, I saw he was alone inside. Down the aisle, Jasmine had Phoenix in crossties while she

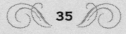

groomed him. She peered under the gray gelding's neck and looked at Julia and Alison, who were filling their horses' water buckets. Julia laughed when Trix, her bay mare, lipped at the hose and sent a spray of water into the air.

I stopped and watched as Jas put down Phoenix's body brush and walked over to Julia and Alison. Jas's confident stride faltered when two-thirds of the Trio stopped giggling and glared at her.

"What do *you* want?" Julia snapped, brushing a lock of her blond bob out of her face.

Alison folded her arms. "Yeah, don't you have someone else to bother?"

I cringed a little for Jasmine.

"I was just saying hi," Jasmine said. "Is Heather around?"

Julia stepped forward. "That is so none of your business. And if you don't stay away from her, we'll make sure you go back to Wellington."

Jasmine paused before she lifted her chin into the air. "Wow," she said. "Insecure much?"

She turned away from them and saw me. I hurried down the aisle, passing her and Phoenix. I felt her eyes burning my back as I went to Charm's stall. I clipped a lead line to his halter and led him in the opposite direction of Phoenix.

"I've got to hurry, boy. Sorry," I said. "Gotta get to class."

Charm snorted and stared at me. He knew that wasn't true. I just wanted to get out of there before I saw Callie. Ignoring Charm's knowing gaze, I picked his hooves and whisked the body brush over him. No Callie. I unclipped him and we went back to his stall. Still no Callie. I gave Charm fresh hay, clean water, and a few scoops of grain. Callie never appeared.

"See you later," I told Charm, kissing his muzzle. He popped his head over the stall door and watched me walk away.

I'd really expected Callie to come find me the second I got to the stable. Didn't she feel like she had to apologize again for going behind my back with Jacob?

An hour later, I took my seat in bio class. Julia turned around to look at me.

"I did *not* miss this class over break," she said.

"Me either," Alison agreed.

Bio wasn't my fave class and most (read: all) of the time, I wasn't thrilled to share the class with Julia and Alison. But today I actually wanted to talk to them.

I leaned forward in my seat. My eyes flickered over

Alison's notebook and I saw a sketch of an Arabian standing proudly with a raised tail—just like Sunstruck. The gorgeous drawing was gallery worthy. Alison closed the notebook when she caught me staring.

"So what's the deal with Jasmine?" I asked. "Do you think she's really trying to make friends?"

Alison smirked. "Puh-lease. She wants to get into our group, learn our secrets, and find a way to get back at Heather for beating her at the regionals. Not gonna happen."

"Yeah, it's obvi that she's still after Heather," Julia said.

The classroom door opened, and Julia and Alison turned back to face the whiteboard. Ms. Peterson, our always tough teacher, stepped inside.

Followed by none other than *Jasmine*.

"No. Way," Alison muttered.

"Class," Ms. Peterson said. "I'd like you to welcome a new student—Jasmine King. Jasmine just transferred from Wellington Preparatory."

Jasmine smiled shyly at the class, looking every bit the scared new girl. She should totally sign up for drama class.

"She is starting late in the year," Ms. Peterson

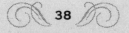

continued. "So I expect all of you to offer her help if she needs it. Jasmine, go ahead and choose an empty seat."

Jasmine's eyes landed on my face. Seriously?! No! But she practically skipped across the room and slid into the seat next to mine. She tossed her loose dark curls over her shoulder and grinned.

I opened my notebook, ignoring her. Wasn't it enough that she lived in Winchester?

"Jasmine?" Ms. Peterson asked. "Did you pick up your books yet?"

"I was so excited this morning that I got there too early and the bookstore was closed," Jas said sweetly. "Then I left right away for class so I wouldn't be a second late on my first day."

In front of me, Alison choked back a snort.

Jasmine = fake.

"All right," Ms. Peterson said. "Well, you may share books with Sasha for today."

I knew Ms. Peterson secretly hated me. I slumped in my seat.

Jasmine scooted her chair closer to mine and leaned over my book. Her lilac-scented body spray made my nose itch, and I inched away from her. This was going to be the longest class *ever*.

*

Once classes were over for the day, Paige and I met up back in our room to rehash.

"What awful things did Jas do in bio class?" Paige asked.

"Nothing," I said. "That's the problem. All of the teachers think she's perfect because she never does anything mean when they're around."

"She's good," she agreed. "But maybe she'll have her books tomorrow and you won't have to share."

"Hopefully. She'll probably get there 'too early' again." I slammed my math book shut for emphasis.

Paige looked up from her desk, where she was doing homework. "Stuck?"

"No, I just feel like riding Charm right now and I can't. It's not fair. I bet Jasmine is riding right now."

"Can't you do something else with Charm? He loves hanging out with you."

I nodded, thinking. "I could walk him. Maybe on the trails."

"Oh! Can I come?" Paige asked, swiveling in her desk chair to look at me. "I've never been on the horse trails."

"Really? I'd love that! Let's go before it gets dark."

We got up and pulled on coats, hats, and scarves. Paige

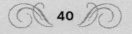

started to grab a pair of furry snow boots, but I shook my head.

"You need these," I said, pointing to my spare pair of paddock boots. "In case Charm steps on you." It was one of the many times I'd been thankful that Paige and I shared a shoe size.

Paige's eyes widened as she took the boots. "*Steps . . . on . . . me?*"

"He won't. Promise," I said. This was exactly what I needed—a walk with both of my best friends.

6

ALMOST KISS
AND TELL

I LOVED SHOWING PAIGE AROUND THE STABLE.
She'd been there before, but this time I explained what
the important things were as we went along. Now Paige
knew about mounting blocks, tie rings, and tack trunks.
We stopped by the tack room to grab Charm's gear, and
then I took Paige to his stall.

"I'm going to clip the lead line to his halter and bring
him out," I told Paige.

She nodded and watched as I led Charm down the aisle
and clipped him into the ties.

"All right, fabulous assistant," I said to Paige.

She grinned and jokingly bowed. "Yes, wise
teacher?"

"I'm going to show you how to groom a horse.

This"—I pointed—"is a tack box. It has all of Charm's brushes and his hoof pick."

"Tack box." Paige nodded. "Got it."

"So, we pick his hooves first. I'll show you, then you can help me."

I grabbed the hoof pick, patted Charm's shoulder, and ran my hand down his leg.

"You squeeze here," I said to Paige. My hand hovered above Charm's fetlock. "Say, 'hoof,' and he'll lift it." On cue, Charm raised his hoof. I scraped the sole, and clods of dirt and sawdust fell to the aisle floor. Paige peered over my shoulder, watching carefully.

"Does that hurt him?" Paige asked.

"Nope," I said. "If you jammed the pick in the frog, that V-shaped part, it would. But the rest of the hoof is pretty tough. Charm's never had a hoof injury."

I lowered Charm's hoof to the ground and walked around to his other foreleg.

"Your turn," I said.

"It's okay. I don't want to mess up his hoof." Paige stuck her hands in her coat pockets.

"You won't. I'll help you."

Paige swallowed. "'Kay."

She stepped up to Charm's side and rubbed his

shoulder. "Remember, you like me," she told Charm.

Her fingers shook as she slid her hand down Charm's leg. "Like this?" she asked.

"Yep. Squeeze right there. He'll lift his hoof and you'll hold his leg."

Paige nodded. "Hoof," she said, squeezing above Charm's fetlock.

Charm raised his hoof off the ground and Paige, totally ready, held up his leg.

"Perfect!" I cheered. "Now face the pick away from you and scrape out the dirt."

Paige cleaned Charm's hoof until it was free of debris, then set it gently on the ground.

"Yay!" Paige said, high-fiving me. "I did it!"

"That's it," I teased. "You're coming with me every morning to do hooves."

Paige nodded. "I'm Charm's new manicurist."

I grinned and tossed her a comb. "You're about to become a hairstylist."

Once Paige had brushed Charm's coat to a pretty gleam, I tossed a kelly green blanket over him.

"Let's go," I said. Paige walked beside me as I led Charm down the aisle and out of the stable. He pointed his ears forward, his breath forming tiny clouds in the cold air.

"Is it bad that it's only Monday and we're already avoiding homework by playing with horses?" Paige asked. I could tell she was already much more comfortable with Charm.

I laughed. "Kinda. But—" I closed my mouth. Callie was walking toward us. She had on a black bomber jacket, jeans, and a deep purple scarf. The scarf I'd given her just days before the Sweetheart Soirée.

Callie's eyes darted back and forth—first looking at Paige and then at me. "Where are you guys going?" she asked.

I shrugged. Paige, making an apologetic face at me, turned to Callie. "We're taking Charm for a walk on the trails," Paige said.

"Oh, good idea," Callie said. "Do you—"

I pulled Charm forward before Callie could finish her sentence. Paige hurried after me and didn't say anything, and we walked in silence until we reached the woods.

The trees and rocks glistened with melting snow. It was different from the dirty, stepped-on campus snow. This snow was blinding white without a footprint anywhere. Birds twittered all around and I half expected to see a deer or fox around every bend in the trail. Callie and

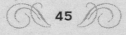

I had ridden up to several deer when we'd . . . I shook the memory out of my head.

"It's pretty out here," Paige said softly. She walked beside me as I led Charm.

"And safe," I said. "No Jasmine. Or Trio. Or Callie."

"I'm sorry I talked to her, but it's sort of weird for me," Paige said.

I sighed. "I know. It's okay. Callie's your friend."

Paige bumped my shoulder with hers. "But you're my *best* friend."

"Was that ever a question?" I teased, smiling.

I thought about what Paige had just said. She was my best friend, but Callie had been my best-best friend. Was Paige my BFF now?

We walked down the dirt path that snaked past the creek. Clear water flowed over the pebble creek bed, and the sound of water rushing around the rocks made me feel more calm. It was like one of those relaxation CDs.

"I know Callie hurt your feelings," Paige said. "But she looks really sad. And so do you."

"I know, but what am I supposed to do? She started dating Jacob before we even officially broke up. How could she do that to me?"

"Do you want Jacob back?" Paige asked.

I led Charm forward a few more steps, thinking about this. "No," I said honestly.

"Sure?" Paige tilted her head and looked at me.

I pointed to a few small boulders by the creek's bank. "Let's sit for a sec."

"Okay . . . but you're making me nervous," Paige said. We sat across from each other, and Charm stood beside me. The clear creek water flowed around the rocks. I made a mental note to bring Eric here—especially after a snowfall. The cold air gave me goose bumps as I perched on the edge of the icy rock, taking a breath.

"I don't want Jacob back because I like someone else," I said.

Paige smiled. "Thought so. Should I guess?"

"I know, I know," I said. "You know it's Eric."

Paige squealed. "He's always been there for you. He's a really good guy. And cute!"

"He really is and I just realized it on Saturday. And . . ." I paused for suspense. "He tried to kiss me!"

Paige almost fell off her rock. "Omigod! What?!"

"He was totally going to kiss me after the clinic, but Mr. Conner almost caught us."

"He really tried to kiss you?!" Paige jumped up and stared at me with her mouth open.

I grinned. "Yes! But then he had to go help Mr. Conner and we haven't had *the* moment again."

Paige sat down and rested her chin on her cupped hand. She sighed. "You almost kissed Eric. Oh. My. God. We have to prep you!"

"I know. You have to help me find kissing gloss." I loosened my scarf.

"I totally will. Promise." Paige caught my eye and we grinned.

"We're so going online shopping the second we get back to Winchester," I said.

We laughed and Charm stuck his head between us, eager not to miss a minute of our conversation.

"That's why I don't want Jacob back," I said. "Eric's good for me, and I really like him. He'd never hurt me like Jacob did. And . . . I'm excited to see what happens. That's why I want everything with Eric to be a secret for a while."

"What do you mean?" Paige shifted on the rock and wrapped her arms across her chest.

"Everyone knew about Jacob and me too early. Heather started plotting against us the second she found out. We didn't even have much time to get to know each other before everything got all messed up."

"She did make things hard, but it was Jacob's fault

too," Paige said. "He didn't do much to reassure you that he wasn't with Heather. And he ignored you when you tried to apologize."

"I know."

Charm stepped closer to me and shoved his muzzle into my hands. His whiskers tickled my palm.

"*He's* not pushy at all," Paige said, laughing. "You know, I think keeping Eric to yourself for a little while might be a good idea."

"It'll give me time to figure out what things are like with him," I said. "It's less pressure and I won't have to worry about anyone sabotaging anything."

"My lips are sealed."

"I know." I smiled at Paige. "I'm *so* glad I told you. And I'm serious about needing your help on my lip gloss search."

Paige shook her head. "So *that's* why you told me!"

"Of course. Kissing gloss is totally different than regular gloss."

We laughed and hunched down in our coats when a chilly wind started to blow.

"If we don't go back soon," I said. "I'll freeze before my first kiss!"

"Now *that*"—Paige's tone was mock-serious—"would be tragic."

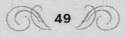

7

SWEET SHOPPE
SHOWDOWN

IT WAS OFFICIAL: NEXT THURSDAY—THE DAY I could ride again—was *never* going to come. There were still eight days left and I didn't know if I'd be able to make it. But Charm was definitely benefitting—I'd channeled all my energy into grooming and walking him. He'd never looked so shiny.

"Bye, Charm," I said, waving to him as I left his stall.

I passed the indoor arena and stopped to look inside. Mr. Conner had five of the intermediate riders, including Eric and Jasmine, trotting their horses around him. I smiled with pride when I watched Eric post on the correct lead and keep his hands down. His dark eyes were narrowed between Luna's ears and he was completely focused.

I shifted my gaze to Jasmine. As hard as it was to admit,

she never belonged on the intermediate team. Everything about the way she rode screamed "advanced." She could have taught the intermediate lesson. Her posture, her signals to Phoenix, and the way she moved with him made everyone else look as if they'd just started riding five minutes ago.

Watching them made me ache to ride Charm. The second the riding ban was lifted, I had to start practicing. Every second I wasted while I couldn't ride, Jasmine inched closer to becoming the best equestrian at Canterwood.

Later that afternoon I stopped by the Sweet Shoppe for my midweek cookie break. I definitely needed a pick-me-up to get through the crazy week. Paige, swamped with homework, had asked me to bring her back a surprise.

I chose four lemon-raspberry cookies and a mint hot chocolate. The Sweet Shoppe was packed, but I spotted a tiny table near the window that faced the courtyard and took a seat just as the Trio entered the shoppe.

Heather whispered something to Julia and Alison, who nodded and got in line. Heather folded her coat over her arm, walked over to my table, and stared down at me.

"You going to be here awhile, or what?" she asked.

I took a sloooow sip of hot cocoa. "Why?"

Heather rolled her eyes. "Because the tables are full. Can't you eat in Winchester? Or the stable?"

"Nooo. But you can go eat in Orchard. Or the stable."

Heather jutted out her chin. "Forget it, Silver. I'll go make someone else move."

I watched as she walked over to a table of sixth graders. They all looked up at her with the same terrified expression. She leaned down, whispered something, and gave them a scary-sweet smile. Within seconds, the girls had gathered their stuff and left. Heather, looking at me from across the room, grinned. She was good.

I turned back to the window and squinted at two people—a boy and a girl—at the edge of the courtyard. The girl skipped a few steps ahead, but she was holding the boy's hand and tugged him with her. Oh, my God. I closed my eyes and reopened them. Callie and Jacob. I wanted to look away, but I couldn't. Callie, laughing, pulled Jacob toward the Sweet Shoppe. As they started up the sidewalk, I looked around for another way out, but I was trapped. I ducked my head as they walked inside. Maybe they wouldn't see me.

As Callie and Jacob approached the counter to order, the bell on the door dinged again and Jasmine stepped

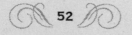

inside. Maybe Heather had been right—I should have just taken my food and left!

Jasmine started toward the counter, but then she looked around and her eyes settled on the Trio's table.

Jasmine weaved around the other tables and stopped in front of Heather, Julia, and Alison. I turned to watch, forgetting about Callie and Jacob for a minute. Hadn't Jasmine gotten enough rejection from the Trio?

The Trio—whose heads were bent together—stopped talking and looked up at Jasmine.

"Can we help you?" Julia asked, rolling her eyes.

Jasmine, not rattled by Julia, smiled. "Just saying hi. You guys hang out here much?"

Alison, Julia, and Heather exchanged is-she-really-talking-to-us glances.

"We're only here now because we can't ride," Julia said. "But we'll be able to soon. Then you'll go back to looking like the loser rider you really are."

Jasmine's head jerked back a fraction.

I cringed. Harsh. Even for Julia. I watched Alison bite her lip—maybe she was thinking the same thing.

"Julia," Heather reprimanded. "Let Jasmine talk."

Julia and Alison looked at each other, then back at Heather. Julia started to open her mouth but stopped.

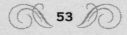

Jasmine gave a slight smirk. "It's totally unfair that you guys can't ride. Maybe we could see a movie or something instead."

Heather smiled at Jas. Julia's and Alison's eyes widened and they both paled.

I couldn't believe it. Heather was going to invite Jasmine into the Trio and then I'd have *four* of them—all on the same side—to deal with. The Quartet. Shudder.

"We'd love to see a movie with you," Heather said. "But we're going to be busy tonight."

Jasmine nodded. "Sure, it was last minute anyway. Maybe tomorrow or something."

Heather pushed back her chair and stood. Behind her back, Julia and Alison froze. Alison looked like she wanted to be anywhere but here. They looked the way I felt— terrified that Heather was about to become Jasmine's friend.

"'Tomorrow or something' doesn't work for us," Heather said. "Because even by tomorrow, we'll still be busy talking about what a pathetic suck-up you are."

Julia and Alison grinned. The Sweet Shoppe—noisy with chatter seconds ago—went silent. Even Callie and Jacob watched. The Belles, who had been sitting at a booth in the back, lifted their heads to see what was going on.

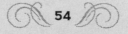

Jasmine's casual posture went rigid.

"Look," Jasmine said. "I know none of us have ever been friends, but we're all at Canterwood now. Don't you think—"

"Let's clear something up, 'kay?" Heather asked in a loud, fake-sweet voice.

"Heather—" Jas started.

But Heather shook her head. "Um, I think I was talking. You've done nothing but try to suck up to everyone since you got here. What? Did you think that just because you go to *our* school now, we'd forget everything and be BFFs?"

"But can't we—" Jasmine started before Heather cut her off.

"What? Start over? Please." Heather stared for several long, uncomfortable seconds. "I know exactly what you're doing. You want to be friends so we'll forget about what you did and leave you alone. Well, guess what?"

Jasmine swallowed. And so did I.

"Not gonna happen," Heather said. "You've done too many shady things to me, my friends, and . . ." Heather sighed and rolled her eyes. "Our team. You will *never* be our friend, so get a life and find someone else to bother. Got it?"

Jasmine's face turned Bubble Yum pink. She spun away from Heather and almost slammed into Callie and Jacob as she hurried for the door. They moved out of the way quickly to let Jas make her exit, and then followed her out. I slumped in my seat, feeling less happy than I thought I would to see Jas leveled like that. Everyone's eyes were on Heather as she smiled and took her seat. I half expected her to bow. She, Julia, and Alison went back to laughing and whispering as if nothing had happened.

Uneasiness gripped my stomach as I watched the Trio laugh. Jasmine didn't like them on a normal day, but now she had another reason to want to take them down.

8

S & S SPLIT

FOR ONCE, I WASN'T LOOKING FORWARD TO film class. It used to be my favorite because I got to sit next to Jacob, but now it was my least favorite for the exact same reason. Assigned seats were the worst; it would be Jacob and me, right next to each other, *every* Friday.

I took my time walking to the media center. Today, Mr. Ramirez was supposed to announce the team grades for our student films. Jacob and I had been partners. Of course. I'd been beyond excited when Mr. Ramirez put us together, and we'd had a lot of fun shooting the film. But now I couldn't even talk to him.

I walked through the lobby, entered the theater, and sank into my plush red seat. Class started in less than two minutes and Jacob still wasn't there. Mr. Ramirez walked to the front of the room, shuffling through a stack of papers. Finally, Jacob walked in and took his seat next to me. He wore a blue striped shirt that I'd never seen before and his hair was pushed off to the side. I couldn't help wondering if he wore it that way because Callie preferred it.

I looked away before Jacob could notice me staring. He leaned forward, pulling out his notebook, and kept his eyes straight ahead.

"Crazy that film's back to Fridays," he said finally.

I shrugged. "Whatever. Better than Mondays."

Mr. Ramirez walked to the front of the room and smiled. He always started film class with a movie quote and it was like a class competition to get the right answer first.

"'There's no place like home,'" Mr. Ramirez said.

Easy!

"*The*—" I started.

"*The Wizard of Oz*," Jacob said, cutting me off. He didn't even give me a sorry-for-cutting-you-off glance. Rude.

"Correct, Jacob," Mr. Ramirez said. "Good job. Now, let's discuss your films. You all submitted excellent, detailed work. I enjoyed viewing each film."

I looked over at Jacob for a second and caught him

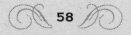

staring at me. Oops. I shifted in my seat, my attention back on Mr. Ramirez.

"I've chosen a few of your films to discuss," Mr. Ramirez said. "Let's start with Brandon and Wes, who produced a comedy."

My phone buzzed. I kept one eye on Mr. Ramirez as I pulled it out of my pocket. It was a text from Eric. Even before I read it, I smiled.

IM ltr, coach?

Jacob shifted in his seat. I jabbed my finger on the off button and dropped my phone into my book bag. Neither of us looked at each other.

"Next," Mr. Ramirez was saying. "An excellent documentary by Jacob and Sasha."

I froze. Before the mess with Jacob, I would have loved Mr. Ramirez talking about our project. But now it was just weird. I didn't want more attention on Jacob and me.

"Jacob and Sasha went on location to Canterwood's stable," Mr. Ramirez said, nodding to us. "They used Sasha's horse, Charm, to show an animal's intelligence. Sasha did most of the on-screen work while Jacob did editing and scoring."

I looked over at Jacob and he glanced back. We traded awkward looks.

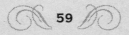

"I'm going to share a clip of the film," Mr. Ramirez said.

The screen went black and the credits started.

S&S presents an original major motion picture. Starring Sasha Silver, Jacob Schwartz, and Charm. Directed by Jacob Schwartz.

I appeared on the giant screen. "Ever wonder how smart animals really are?" I asked.

I slid into my seat, shielding my eyes with my hands. This was *so* embarrassing! I talked for few more seconds, and then on-camera, Jacob walked over to me. He'd been terrified of Charm, I'd later found out; he was afraid of horses—but he'd gone along with the horse-themed documentary for me. I forced myself to watch on-camera Jacob and not the real one.

"Sasha and Jacob worked as partners and demonstrated the teamwork that's necessary to be successful in the film industry." Mr. Ramirez smiled and tipped his head to us. "I hope both of you consider making more films together in the future."

Jacob and I just nodded. I slumped into my seat with relief when Mr. Ramirez chose the next movie. Mr. R had no idea that *Horse Sense* was the last project Jacob and I would ever do together.

When class finally ended, I stuffed my notebook into

my bag. Jacob shifted toward me for a second, his eyes on my face. I thought he might say something, but he only shook his head and got up. He disappeared down the aisle before I even squeezed out of our row.

9

WANNA SEE
A REAL RIDER?

"THERE," I SAID, SLAMMING MY HISTORY BOOK
closed. "Weekend homework is done."

I shoved my chair back from my desk and stretched.
The weekend had been too short. I'd been busy walking Charm, doing Canterwood's infamous never-ending
homework, and breaking once in a while for TV time with
Paige. She'd distracted me from missing Eric yesterday.
He'd gone off campus for a field trip to a natural history
museum. So Paige and I had made it through the fifth disc
of the new season of *City Girls*—Paige's new obsession.
Now I was addicted too.

"Finally," Paige said. "And tomorrow, lucky us, we start
the week all over again."

I groaned. "Thanks for the reminder."

"But at least Eric's back today," Paige said.

I smiled. "I know."

Paige thought for a second. "Hmm. We totally need to shop for lip gloss. You know Eric's going to try to kiss you again."

I sat up straighter. "I totally forgot about kissing gloss!"

Paige grabbed her laptop and pulled it onto her lap as she sat on her bed. "C'mon. Let's hit Sephora and Bonne Bell."

I settled beside Paige and peered at her laptop screen. "I think I need something with shine *and* color," I said. "But nothing sticky."

Paige clicked through Bonne Bell website. We scrolled through dozens of glosses before Paige stopped. "This one," she said. "Sheer Kiwi. It's pink but not too pink. It's shiny but doesn't look gooey."

"Oooh, get it," I said.

Paige added the gloss to my cart and we kept shopping. We added berry flavors, ice cream flavors, and even vanilla-chocolate swirl.

"But . . ." I paused, thinking about how dumb my question was going to sound. "What if he doesn't like the flavor? What if I get raspberry and he hates raspberries?"

Paige patted my arm. "He won't care about the flavor, trust me. He'll just want to kiss you. But if you're worried, then let's pick some safe ones. Like mint, or something."

"Okay," I said. Paige found spearmint, peppermint, and unscented shine (boring!) and I ordered them—overnight shipping just in case Eric tried to kiss me sooner rather than later.

"You've definitely got enough gloss," Paige said. "Now you're prepared."

I nodded, but there were still bubbles in my stomach. Even though I had enough lip gloss for lots of kisses, I still didn't know *how* to kiss.

Buzzz. I grabbed my phone.

Stable soon?

Eric's text made me grin.

4 sure! C u in 20.

Paige looked at me and laughed. "Hmm, wonder who that was?"

"No one!" I covered my blushing face with my hands.

"Oh, yeah, it's not obvious at all," Paige teased.

I bounced off my bed and walked to my closet. "Fiiine. I'm going to see Eric. Happy?"

Paige nodded. "Very." She got up from her desk and

flopped on her bed. "And wear your pink sweater. It'll look cute with black breeches."

"Oooh, good idea." I pulled the clothes from my closet and got dressed. I applied a light coat of Bonne Bell Lip Glam in my fave new shade—Brown Sugar Shine. Mmm.

"Hair?" I called to Paige. "Down or up?"

"Down," Paige said.

I brushed my hair, misted it with shine spray, and stood in front of Paige.

"Do I look okay?" I asked.

"Perfect. But don't kiss in front of the horses. They're too impressionable."

"Ha, ha," I said, rolling my eyes at her as I grabbed a coat and left our room.

I headed for Charm's stall. He would be the perfect company while I waited for Eric.

But steps away from Charm's stall, my pace slowed. Callie stood in front of the stall door, touching Charm's cheek. Silver bangles flashed on her wrist.

She looked at me and took a half step in my direction, rubbing her hands on the front of her tan breeches. She'd probably worn them out of habit too. "I've been waiting awhile. I wanted to stay till you showed up."

"Why?"

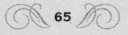

Charm strained his head toward me, begging me to come over and pet him, but I didn't move.

"Because we have to talk. I need to apologize, Sasha. You don't have to forgive me, but . . ."

I squeezed my eyes shut for a second, trying not to cry. I hated this—all of it. If only I could forget everything that had happened with Callie and Jacob. Callie and I could go back to being best friends, we'd prep for the YENT tryouts together, and things wouldn't be weird between us. But I couldn't forget and I didn't know how long it would take for me to be able to let Callie explain.

"I can't do this right now," I said. "And you have to stop trying to make me. Remember when you wouldn't let me explain about Eric, no matter how many times *I* apologized?"

Callie swallowed. "I know, but—"

"I've gotta go."

I left Callie standing there, staring after me, and walked away. I missed her and hoped we could be friends some day, but she'd hurt me. And for now I didn't know what to do about that.

Inside the indoor arena, I paced the dirt floor while I waited for Eric. He walked in, leading Luna, a few minutes later. Just seeing him made me feel better. And I didn't

want him to see me upset about Callie, so I hid it with a smile.

"Hey, Coach Silver," Eric called.

"Hello, number one student."

Eric flashed a smile that made me forget all about Callie. "You sure you don't have another favorite student?"

"Like?"

Eric shrugged and pulled down a stirrup. "C'mon. I know. You're out here giving riding lessons to your best friend Jasmine in the middle of the night."

I laughed. "You caught me. Jas is the *best* student ever. You, though, are impossible to teach."

We grinned at each other as Eric put on his helmet and mounted.

After Luna was warmed up, I asked Eric to do a couple of exercises, including my personal favorite (not!), posting without stirrups. But Eric didn't argue—he knew he needed the work.

I watched and tried not to grin at the expression on Eric's face. He was trying to act as if he didn't feel like his legs were about to fall off. But he was totally in pain! I motioned for him to slow Luna and he shot me a look.

I put my hands on my hips. "Fine. Just for that, I'm going to make you jump the long course."

Eric did that "'Sup," head-bobbing thing guys do, like it was a challenge. "Whatever. Let's do it."

Then he winked at me. I forced myself not to swoon and tried to keep a neutral look on my face. I wasn't going to be a dork in front of him. But the second he turned Luna away from me, I almost crumpled to the floor. My cheeks were hot and my chest felt tingly. I took a couple of deep breaths and put my cool hands on my face, trying to stop the flush.

Eric turned back to me and I yanked my hands down and smiled. *Stop blushing,* I yelled to myself. I couldn't let Eric think I was one of those giggly OMG-a-guy-likes-me girls.

Luna threw up her head and sidestepped when Eric asked her to trot. He took her away from the jump course and trotted her along the wall, calming her with his hands and legs. He knew how to speak to her without ever saying anything. That wasn't easy. Eric was a fairly new rider, but sometimes he looked as if he'd been on horses his whole life. He was so—

"Ahh!" I yelled. Jasmine had materialized next to me. "Say something next time!"

She rolled her eyes. "Chill."

Eric looked over, saw Jasmine, then focused again on Luna.

"What's with you?" I asked. I wanted to smack myself when I realized how much I craved the long black one-button cardigan Jasmine wore over her breeches.

"Nothing," she said.

We watched Eric take Luna through figure eights. Maybe Jas was checking out the competition.

"You must really like him," Jasmine said.

"What?" I asked. "Who?"

She rolled her eyes. "Eric. Because he's an *intermediate* rider. Why else would you waste your time?"

"Helping someone is not wasting time. And anyway, you're an intermediate rider too, remember?"

Jasmine's smirk slipped. "Not for long."

Eric turned Luna toward the course. Perfect timing. I knew they hadn't jumped much in Eric's intermediate class, and if he rode now like he had during our last lesson, Jas would freak!

Eric pointed Luna toward the first green and gold vertical. Beside me, Jas yawned. Luna leaped over the jump in perfect form and Eric let her out a notch, rocking with her canter.

Yes! Go Eric! I cheered to myself. I looked at Jasmine and fought the urge to say, "Told you."

Luna started toward the faux-brush jump. Eric's

timing was amazing as he squeezed his legs against Luna. She popped over the brush jump, the oxer, and the tall vertical. Eric didn't lose concentration for a second, and he looked as if he'd been practicing with Luna for years. I forced myself not to turn into a cheerleader.

Jasmine craned her neck to see. Her gaze narrowed and her eyes followed Eric over every jump until she caught me watching her. "Whatever," she said, shrugging. "It's a fluke. He never rides this well in class."

"'Kay," I said. "If you say so."

But Jasmine didn't stop watching. She pouted a little more with every jump Luna cleared. Luna thundered over the final vertical and Eric slowed her to a trot. He started toward us and couldn't hide his grin.

"Awesome," I said. "You killed it."

Eric shrugged modestly. "We could still use some more practice."

"Well, you're not doing it now," Jasmine snapped. "I have a private lesson with Mr. Conner. He's prepping me for my advanced team test. I'm not going to be stuck on the dumb intermediate team much longer."

"Okay," Eric said lightly. He dismounted and turned to Jasmine. "Have a good ride."

He was always so calm with Jas. I wished I could be as

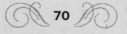

calm—whenever she acted like this, it made me want to scream.

"You should stay if you want to see what real riding looks like," Jasmine said.

"Thanks, but I've seen Sasha ride before," Eric said. "See ya in class."

Omigod! Best. Line. Ever. I struggled not to grin at the expression on Jas's face.

10

SO NOT A
LUNCH DATE

ON TUESDAY, I TOOK MY SEAT IN BIO CLASS
feeling panicky. I'd spent waaay too much time on IM with
Eric the night before and hadn't prepped for today's likely
pop quiz, but IMing had been *so* much fun. We'd talked
about riding, how lame TV shows were right now, and the
look on Jasmine's face when Eric finished his ride. Eric
hadn't tried to kiss me again and I was kind of relieved. I
hadn't read enough Kissing 101 articles in *TweenGirl* yet.

In the seat across from me, Jasmine was texting.

Julia and Alison sauntered into the classroom and sat in
front of me. Alison turned around to face me and flipped
her messy French braid over her shoulder.

"If I don't ride soon," she said, "I'm going to die."

"Me too," I admitted.

Julia turned around and smoothed her A-line skirt. "We just have to make it till Thursday," she said. "Then it's *on*."

"I'll have to ride, like, every second to catch up," Alison said.

"Yeah, but what about history?" Julia asked. She opened her yellow notebook covered with faint *I ♥ Ben* scribbles. "It's killing us *now* and we're not even riding. Mr. Fields is *so* ridic with all of the homework!"

Jasmine glanced up from texting, and her eyes wandered to Julia and Alison.

"Were we talking to you?" Julia hissed.

Jas rolled her eyes and started rummaging through her bag. Julia and Alison turned around, whispering to each other. Alison almost looked like she felt sorry for Jasmine. Almost.

I looked down at my notes and tried to shut out everything around me. I wasn't going to mess up my grades when I was so close to getting my riding privileges back. But it wasn't easy—no matter how hard I tried to focus on bio, my mind always wandered to Eric and the way it had felt to IM with him last night. A great guy actually wanted to talk to me. He could have played video games or hung out with his friends, but he wanted to IM. With me.

*

At lunchtime I bolted for the cafeteria. *Be cool*, I told my-self. I reminded myself that it had to look like Eric and I were friends. I got in the lunch line and piled my tray with a hot dog, mac and cheese, and applesauce. A quick scan of the lunchroom told me that Eric wasn't there yet, so I picked a table near the back and waited for him.

Heather, flanked by Julia and Alison, walked in and they took their usual table at the center of the caf.

I started to wave at Eric when I saw him walk through the doors, but then I put my hand down. Waving would have been too obvious, right?

Once Eric reached the table, he set his tray across from mine. "Is it really only Tuesday?" he asked.

"Long day?"

Eric nodded and popped a French fry into this mouth. "*So* long. I kind of felt like lunch would never get here."

I smiled, trying not to blush. "Me too."

I bit into my hot dog, but almost choked when I looked across the cafeteria. Callie and Jacob were holding hands, headed for the lunch line. I'd never seen Callie so dressed up for class. She had on a shrunken black blazer, a fitted scoop-neck sweater, and tall boots with a slight heel.

"So I told Troy that he . . ." Eric said, but I barely

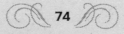

heard him. I couldn't stop watching Callie and Jacob. Callie laughed at something Jacob said as they searched for a table. She saw me, though, and her smile wavered. She took a couple of steps toward our table, then stopped. I could almost feel her trying to decide what to do. We used to have so much fun at lunch. Giggling, gossiping, swapping stable stories. But it was Callie's fault that it wasn't like that anymore. She looked away from me when Jacob pointed to an empty table by the window. Callie followed him, not glancing back.

"Sasha?"

"Huh?" I tore my gaze away from Callie and Jacob.

Eric waved a hand in front of my face. "You okay?"

"Fine, sorry," I said. "I-I just spaced out for a sec."

Eric nodded. "It's okay."

"What were you saying?" I asked.

"Oh, I just told Troy that he didn't need a new saddle pad—he just had to wash his for once."

I nodded, feigning interest. "Oh. Yeah. His old one is fine."

Eric talked for a few minutes about Troy's tack, and I tried to pay attention, but my focus drifted to the Trio's table.

In the center of the room, I saw that Heather, Julia, and

Alison were laughing, their eyes on Jasmine. She sat with her back to them, listening to her iPod. Heather shifted in her chair, her gaze on Jas. The Trio was up to something.

"Turn around," I whispered to Eric. "But don't look obvious."

Eric shifted, and his eyes followed my gaze. Heather shoved her chair back, got up, and sauntered over to Jasmine's table. Jasmine didn't even hear her coming.

Heather leaned down, her head almost touching Jasmine's shoulder. Jas yanked out her ear buds and turned to eye Heather.

"Jasmine's freaked," I whispered.

Eric nodded. "She should be."

Heather's lips moved next to Jas's ear, and whatever she said made the former Wellington girl blush.

Heather pushed up the sleeves of her royal blue sweater and tilted her head toward Julia and Alison. Jasmine made a "Whatever" gesture, but Heather continued to stare down at her. It made even *me* squirm. Julia grinned at Jasmine, but Alison looked uncomfortable, tugging at the ends of her long sandy hair. Finally, with a satisfied smirk, Heather walked back to her table.

Eric turned around and shook his head. "That's going to get baaad," he said.

"I know. I'm staying out of it." We went back to our lunch, but I kept an eye on Jasmine. She picked at her food for the rest of the period and—as much as I didn't like her—I started to feel for her.

Whatever just happened, the Trio hadn't even gotten started. I knew, firsthand, what they were capable of.

11

NEVER A DRAMA-FREE MOMENT

AFTER CLASS I CHANGED AND STARTED toward the stable. Looking across the campus, I watched the track team, in their green and gold uniforms, jog around the outdoor track. A brisk wind chilled my fingers and I tried to warm them up by texting Paige while I walked.

Sooo . . . b/c u went 2 that how 2 live green mtg during lunch, u missed big drama!

Paige texted back. *I did??? What?!*

H got in Jas's face & said smthing awful. Jas looked 8-0 when H left.

Uh-oh. Tell me more ltr!

I clicked my phone shut and walked by the indoor arena, peering through the window. Inside, Eric, Troy, and

Ben were trotting their horses. Eric, edging Luna next to Ben's horse, was laughing at whatever Ben had said. I left the window, grabbed Charm's tack box, and went to his stall.

"Hi, Charmy," I said. "Two more days till I can ride."

Charm snorted—he hated it when I called him that. I clipped a lead line to his brown leather halter and led him to a pair of crossties. I took my time grooming him, and Charm loved every second of it, closing his eyes as I brushed him.

"You're not enjoying this at all, I can tell," I teased Charm.

He bobbed his head.

I looked up when I heard hoofbeats approaching. Callie, with Jacob by her side, led Jack down the aisle. Sigh. So much for a drama-free afternoon.

Jack stretched his neck toward his BFF Charm. Jacob stayed in the middle of the aisle, avoiding the horses who stuck their heads over the stall doors. I almost felt sorry for him—his current and ex-almost girlfriends both loved horses and he was so scared of them.

Callie stopped Jack in front of Charm and the two horses touched muzzles. I kept brushing Charm, determined not to look at Callie and Jacob.

"Hi," Callie said, her tone soft.

"Hey," Jacob said.

I glanced at them but didn't say anything.

Callie played with the end of Jack's lead line. "So we get to ride soon. Finally, huh?"

I shrugged.

"I'm glad we at least have time to practice before Jasmine joins our team," Callie added.

"I'd rather ride with Jas," I muttered. I looked away and flicked the brush over Charm's already clean shoulder.

"What?" Callie asked.

My chest twisted a little when I looked at her. I knew what I'd said—and what I was about to say—was wrong. But it didn't stop me.

"Jasmine was never my best friend," I said. "So she could never hurt me the way you did. I expect it from her, but *you*?" My voice cracked, threatening to give away the emotions behind what I'd said.

"It's not all Callie's fault," Jacob interjected.

My arms dropped to my sides and I turned to face them head-on. "So that makes it okay?" I asked.

Callie swallowed and her eyes filled with tears. "I was so, so wrong—I know it. But I miss you, Sash, and I'm trying to explain what happened. Can we go somewhere and talk?"

I tossed Charm's brush into his tack box. It thudded against the other brushes. I unclipped the crossties, letting the snaps clank against the walls.

I backed Charm up, turned him, and led him away. I knew if I said another word, I'd start sobbing. I shouldn't have been mean to Callie. But I meant what I said. Jasmine—annoying as she was—meant nothing to me. Callie had been my best friend.

At that moment, I realized something that hadn't really occurred to me before. This could be it for my and Callie's friendship—maybe it really was beyond repair.

I put Charm away and walked by the indoor arena. Eric was inside, trotting Luna in a circle. He was concentrating so intently that he didn't see me walk into the center of the arena.

"Watch those hands, Mr. Rodriguez," I called out.

Eric's head twisted in my direction. He dropped his hands, laughing.

"Yes, Mr. Conner," he teased.

He rode Luna over to me and dismounted.

"You don't have to stop," I said. "I'm going back to Winchester anyway."

Eric took off his helmet and ran his fingers through his dark hair. "It's okay. I'm pretty much done for the day."

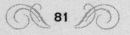

81

I patted Luna, and Eric took a step closer to me. He took my hand. "So," he said. "About that kiss . . ."

Kiss? Was he serious? But I wasn't expecting it yet. I wasn't— But as I stared into his warm brown eyes, my nerves vanished. Eric leaned into me, and my eyes fluttered shut. His lips, soft and warm, touched mine. My worries about being a bad kisser faded instantly; nothing about kissing Eric felt wrong. After he pulled away, Eric brushed a stray hair from my face. He smiled at me.

"I'm really glad you did that," I said, hyperaware that we were still standing so close together.

"Good," he said. "Me too."

I didn't even care that I hadn't put on lip gloss for at least an hour.

12

FIGURES

"OMIGOD!" I SHRIEKED.

"What's wrong?!" Paige whipped back her covers and sat up, her red hair staticky.

I double-checked my phone. Yes! It really was six on Thursday morning. "I get to ride today!" I yelled.

"Oh." Paige flopped back into bed. "Don't do that! I thought something serious was happening. Like a fire. Or the cancellation of *Top Chef*."

"Sorry," I whispered.

I grabbed the riding clothes I'd picked out last night and pulled them on in record time. I swept my hair into a messy ponytail and swiped on some vanilla bean lip gloss.

"Have fun," Paige whispered, half asleep.

"I will. Bye." I opened the door and eased it shut behind me.

The sun, just starting to rise, cast a pink and orange glow over campus. The trees were finally getting their leaves back and the grass was losing its winter brown. I breathed in the chilly air and smiled. Everything looked prettier this morning! Maybe that's because I was Eric's girlfriend. I touched my phone in my pocket. After yesterday's kiss, I'd picked up my phone to tell Callie everything. Then I'd remembered we weren't friends anymore. This was the weirdest semester ever. I'd lost a best friend, lost an almost boyfriend, and now was a date away from becoming someone's official girlfriend.

At the stable, I grabbed Charm's tack box, saddle, pad, and bridle before dashing around the corner to his stall.

"Riding day, boy!" I cheered.

Charm bumped my arm with his head. I barely had time to clip the lead line to his halter before he charged out into the aisle.

"Whoa!" I said, laughing.

But I let him prance down the aisle to the crossties. He barely blinked as I groomed him—he was ready to go!

In less than ten minutes, we were on our way to the

indoor arena. I put my foot in the stirrup and boosted myself into Charm's saddle.

"Ahhh," I said, settling into the leather. The no-riding thing was never happening again. Ever.

I urged Charm forward and we joined the Trio, who was warming up their horses along the wall.

"Seriously, I couldn't sleep last night," Alison said. She patted Sunstruck's palomino shoulder. The Arabian gelding stretched his neck out to Trix, Julia's bay mare.

"Me either," Julia said. "It's crunch time now to make up for those two weeks."

Heather nodded and edged Aristocrat between Trix and Sunstruck. "Not to mention, this will probably be one of our last practices without *her*. If she makes the team, she'll bring us all down."

Heather gazed at me. "Kind of like when you first came to Canterwood. At least you got somewhat better, Silver."

I rolled my eyes. "Gee. Thanks."

Callie and Jack came riding into the arena. She gave us a quick smile, but no one reciprocated. Interesting. Julia and Alison had been Callie's new BFFs when they thought Heather and I had stolen Julia's and Callie's guys. Now they wouldn't even look at her. They'd dropped Callie the

second Julia forgave Heather for dating Ben—Julia's then boyfriend. Everyone's friendships were fixed and back to normal, except for me and Callie's.

We moved our horses to the arena wall and started our warm-up. Callie inched Jack toward Charm a couple of times, but I weaved Charm around the other horses to avoid her. She finally seemed to give up and stayed behind us.

Mr. Conner walked into the arena's center. He looked at us and nodded. "Glad to be back?"

"YES!" we chorused.

Mr. Conner laughed. "Good! Then let's get started. Move out to the wall and trot."

I nudged Charm with my heels and he trotted forward. We fell into line behind Aristocrat. Charm's pace quickened—he wanted to pass his rival. Ahead of us, the darker chestnut increased his speed.

"Not worth it," I whispered to Charm. I got him settled and we finished the warm-up.

"Today, we're practicing dressage," Mr. Conner announced.

Not my fave discipline, since I was all about crosscountry, but I was too excited about riding to care.

"We're going to work on figure eights," Mr. Conner said. He walked to the side of the arena and picked up two orange traffic cones. He placed the cones a few feet apart.

"Why figure eights?" Alison asked.

"Riding this pattern forces you to pay attention to how you sit on your horse," Mr. Conner said. "As your horse shifts directions, you'll feel how you balance yourself to stay in the saddle. The exercise also gives your horse greater flexibility."

Alison nodded and straightened her black helmet. I sneaked a look at Callie—dressage was her favorite exercise. She turned her head to the side, and silver flashed in her ear. I squinted—it was a tiny horseshoe earring. Those were new. We used to do all of our accessory shopping together, so even though I knew it was stupid, seeing Callie's new earrings reminded me of how awful things had gotten and much I missed my old friend.

"Let's begin," Mr. Conner said.

I shrugged off my sadness and made myself pay attention. No distractions.

"Alison, you'll go first. Then Sasha, Callie, Heather, and Julia," Mr. Conner instructed.

"Okay," Alison said.

"Start Sunstruck at a forward trot," Mr. Conner called.

"Squeeze with your legs and lengthen his stride before you begin the pattern."

Alison nodded and eased Sunstruck into a trot. The Arabian was flighty, but Alison knew how to handle him. She circled him twice and then weaved him through the cones. Sunstruck, with his smooth stride, made it easy for Alison to bend with him through the turns. She rode him back to us, and Mr. Conner nodded to her.

"When you ride your horse through the turns," he said, "you should pull back your inside leg while moving your outside leg forward. This will help your horse navigate the twists."

Alison rubbed Sunstruck's neck and the rest of us nodded.

Mr. Conner looked at me. "Go ahead, Sasha."

I trotted Charm forward and, like Alison, asked Charm for two circles before we started the pattern. Shifting in the saddle, I focused on my posture as Charm made the first circle. I shortened the reins, slowing Charm a notch. Charm flowed through the circle and we completed the rest of the figure eight.

"Nice, boy," I whispered, riding him back to the group.

Mr. Conner gave me a rare wide smile. "Excellent, Sasha."

Callie, Heather, and Julia all completed the exercise with ease. They looked as if they'd done figure eights a million times. Mr. Conner made us ride through it for the rest of the lesson.

"Thanks, girls," Mr. Conner said. "See you this afternoon."

We dismounted and led our horses out of the arena. "Great job, boy," I told Charm. I found Mike, my favorite groom, and handed him Charm's reins. "Thanks," I said.

"No prob," Mike said with a smile. "Just glad to have you back in the saddle." He patted Charm's neck before leading him away.

At least some things in my life were finally getting back to normal.

I was just a few doors away from Mr. Davidson's English class when I saw Eric walking down the hallway.

I tried not to bounce up and down when I saw him. He was insanely cute. He wore a gray long-sleeve polo shirt and baggy-but-not-too-baggy vintage-wash jeans. I leaned against the wall, hugging my books to my chest. I had to stop blushing every time I saw him or he'd think I was ridiculous.

"Hi," I said as he approached.

89

Eric smiled. "Hey."

"I rode Charm this morning," I said, grinning.

"That must have felt amazing," Eric said. "How was it?"

I sighed. "So. Good."

"About time, huh?"

"No kidding." I tried not to stare into his amber-flecked brown eyes.

"So, sit with me at lunch?" Eric asked without taking his eyes off mine.

Swoon.

I paused, remembering my vow not to let anyone find out about me and Eric—not to give anyone a chance to mess up something so exciting and perfect. Would anyone suspect we were together if we sat at the same table again? I wondered, but then I realized that Paige would be there too.

"Sure," I said.

Eric smiled. "Good. And you know we have to go on a date soon."

I stopped myself from saying, "YES! A date!"

Instead, I said, "A date?"

"We don't have to," Eric teased.

"I can't wait."

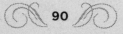

90

"Once we go on a date," Eric said, "you'll officially be my girlfriend. I mean, if you want."

I nodded fervently, my chandelier earrings rattling against my neck. One date stood between old Sasha and girlfriend Sasha. I watched Eric walk down the hallway, and had to try waaay too hard not to follow him. I waited until he disappeared before I turned—and almost smacked right into Jacob!

"Omigod," I said. "What are you doing?"

"Sorry," he said. He reached out a hand to steady me, but pulled back before he touched me. He blushed. "You okay?"

"Fine," I mumbled, turning away.

"Sasha, wait. Are you—"

But I didn't let him finish his question. I darted around him and pulled open the door to Mr. Davidson's class.

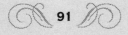

13

TRIO VS. BELLES

BY FRIDAY, ERIC AND I HAD SAT TOGETHER at lunch twice. No one seemed suspicious of us, but I still worried that someone might find out. I wished Eric and I could just sit together and not have to worry about anything. It was stupid that I had to be secretive about something that made me so happy, but every time I thought about letting things out in the open, I remembered Callie and Jacob and thought, *Oh. Right.*

Eric smiled at me as I reached our table. I put down my tray and pretended to stretch. Paige had been a few people behind me in the lunch line. I wanted to wait for her before sitting solo with Eric again.

"You going to eat standing up?" Eric teased.

"No," I said, forcing a laugh. "I'm just...waiting for Paige."

"She won't care if you sit."

"Yeah," I said. "But . . ." I trailed off as I scanned the caf for Paige. I finally saw her and shot her the hurry-up-now eyes.

What? she mouthed.

I shook my head. *Never mind,* I mouthed back.

"Hey," Paige said to Eric. She slid next to him and I sat across from her. "Sorry I was late," Paige said, looking at me. "My *Teen Cuisine* producer called to talk about the summer filming schedule."

"That's so cool," I said. "I'm totally visiting you on set."

Paige smiled, but then Eric's tray caught her attention. Like Paige, Eric liked food. He didn't *cook*, but he always had the best sandwiches for lunch.

Eric pushed his tray over to Paige for inspection. "What do you think?" he asked.

She peered at the sandwich. "Barbecue chicken, right? With smoked honey sauce?"

Eric nodded. "My dad's sauce. He sent it FedEx."

"Smells great," Paige said. "I haven't made many sauces. But I should."

"My roommate used to tease me about my dad's food packages," Eric said. "But when he came into our common room and smelled the chicken, he changed his mind pretty fast."

We laughed. "Of course he did," I said. "He wanted you to share."

The Trio arrived late—like always. And, also like always, they strolled through the center of the cafeteria. Heather, who usually walked between Julia and Alison, actually walked on the outside next to Julia. She balanced a silver lunch tray in her hands—a tray full of *soda*. Four giant glasses, nothing else.

"Heather's carrying a tray of soda," I whispered to Paige and Eric. "New diet?"

Paige sneaked a look over her shoulder. "Dunno. Maybe she's going back for food."

The Trio turned their gazes toward something near the window.

Jasmine.

She sat by herself, her back to them, ear buds in and munching on a sandwich.

Not. Good. She should have learned from her last Heather encounter that iPods in the caf were dangerous.

Julia, Alison, and Heather, still laughing, sashayed over to Jasmine. If their goal was to get everyone to watch, they were succeeding. One by one, heads started popping up as people watched the Trio approach Jasmine.

Even the Belles—Violet, Brianna, and Georgia—glanced up from their lunches. The caf went silent—no clicking of spoons against bowls, no scraping of forks against plates. Nothing. I'd never heard it so quiet.

The Trio shook off their giggles and stopped behind Jas. At Heather's nod, Julia tapped Jas on the shoulder.

Jas jumped, then turned around. She yanked her ear buds out of her ears, and her eyes widened, flicking to the sodas and then to the Trio.

"Jasmine," Heather said brightly. Her voice seemed to echo through the cafeteria.

Jasmine's gaze shifted among Julia, Alison, and Heather. "Hey?" she said. It came out like a question.

"Enjoying your lunch?" Alison asked, nodding at Jasmine's tray.

"Um, sure," Jasmine said. She shifted in her seat. She had to know the Trio was up to something.

"Good!" Julia said. She looked so friendly that, for a second, I thought she'd hug Jasmine.

"Look, we've been talking," Heather said. She smiled, flashing her teeth.

Danger! Danger!

"This situation is just so awkward for everyone," Heather continued.

The entire cafeteria seemed to be hanging on her every word.

Jasmine nodded and her shoulders relaxed. But I knew better. Across from me, Paige and Eric had abandoned their food to watch.

"We've been handling this all wrong," Heather added. She leaned closer to Jasmine.

"Yeah, we're just sorry we waited so long," Julia said.

Jasmine stood, wrapping her arms across her chest. "Omigosh, don't even apologize. Really. I'm just glad we can stop fighting with each other twenty-four/ seven."

Heather nodded, her face serious. "Agreed. We're so done fighting. 'Cause, really, it was about time I did *this*."

Before Jas could even blink, Heather flipped her tray right onto Jasmine. Everyone in the caf sucked in a breath. Soda sloshed though the air between them and soaked Jas. In an instant, her clothes and hair were drenched. The tray and plastic glasses clattered to the floor, landing at Jas's feet. Her lips parted, but she didn't say a word.

I immediately felt sorry for her. She'd done awful things to us, but the Trio had already humiliated her enough. What was the point anymore? But I already knew the answer to that. The point was to never stop making her pay. Almost a year ago, it would have been me on the receiving end of that soda.

"There! I feel *so* much better!" Heather said, smirking. "How does it feel? You poured oil on Aristocrat, and then molasses in Sasha's hair. It was your turn, Jas. Are you ready to crawl back to Wellington yet?"

Jasmine just stood there, dripping soda onto the floor. The cola formed a puddle around her boots. Her face was as white as Charm's blaze.

"Ta!" Heather, Julia, and Alison chirped at the same time. They turned and started out of the cafeteria. They were just about to pass the Belles' table when Violet got up and stood in front of them.

"Hold it," Violet said, folding her arms.

Heather tossed Violet a playful grin. Heather obviously thought that, as a fellow clique leader, Violet would be proud.

But then Violet did something strange. She tucked her light brown, chin-length hair behind her ear and leaned close to Heather. "You're so transparent. It's sad."

Heather straightened. "Whatever. It was just a harm-less little prank."

Violet's eyes narrowed. Heather didn't need to make the Belles mad—they were probably already mad enough at us about the whole banned-from-riding thing.

"The only reason you're going after Jasmine is to secure *your* spot as Canterwood's top seventh-grade rider," Violet said. "And after the way you and your little friends got us in trouble, that's not a spot you deserve."

Heather squirmed. Julia and Alison shifted back on their heels, looking like they wanted to run away. Brianna and Georgia walked over and flanked Violet.

"So either leave Jasmine alone, or we'll come after *you*. Got it?" Violet said.

"Whatever," Heather whispered again.

Violet peered around the Trio at Jasmine. "C'mon," she said.

Jasmine, trying not to slide on the spilled soda, grabbed her bag and skirted the Trio. The Belles formed a protective barrier around Jasmine and walked her out of the caf. The room erupted in chatter the second they disappeared.

Heather, Julia, and Alison didn't move. They stood frozen to the spot where Violet had crushed Heather.

Their faces were pink, and Alison and Julia stared at the ground. Heather, realizing people were looking, tossed her hair over her shoulder and walked out. Julia and Alison hurried out behind her.

Spilling soda on Jas? Biggest. Mistake. Ever.

14

CLUELESS

AFTER MY RIDING LESSON I WALKED TOWARD the stable exit. I had film class tonight—ugh. If only Eric were in my class instead of Jacob. I walked by Jack's stall and saw he was alone inside, munching on a mouthful of hay. When he saw me, he pricked his ears and walked up to the stall door. He stretched his neck to me and I rubbed his cheek.

"I miss you too, boy," I said. "And so does Charm."

I petted Jack, thinking about how many trail rides Callie and I had missed since that awful Saturday. One of my favorite parts of the weekends had been riding with Callie and getting away from the pressure of the advanced team. I had Paige and Eric, but they didn't understand what it was like to be on the advanced team.

"I don't know what to do," I said to Jack.

Jack stared at me with his big brown eyes. He nudged my shoulder and I smoothed his forelock. "See you later, boy."

I left him and ran into Alison at the exit. We walked through the door without saying a word. Usually, Alison would snap at me for walking within a ten-yard radius of her. But she just fell into step beside me. Weird.

"Everything okay?" I asked hesitantly.

Alison shrugged. She transferred her folder from one arm to the other and I saw a sketch of a horse head on the front.

"Pretty," I said, pointing to the drawing.

Alison blushed. "Thanks."

We walked for a few more seconds before she turned her head toward me.

"I guess we shouldn't have done that, huh?" she asked.

"Done what?"

"Poured soda on Jasmine."

I looked up from the sidewalk and stared at Alison. "Maybe not. Heather really, really embarrassed her."

Alison took her hair out of its ponytail. It fell down to the middle of her back, brushing against her green jacket.

"I don't like her or anything, but I shouldn't have gone along with Heather and Julia."

"Why did you?" I braced myself for Alison to huff away.

"Because they're the only friends I have," Alison said. "It's always been Julia, Heather, and me."

We reached the courtyard—the spot where Alison and I would split up to go to our dorms.

"You don't have to go along with them all the time if you don't want to," I said. "And if Heather and Julia get mad, you can make new friends."

"Yeah, like the Belles?" Alison joked. "Hey, at least I'd be in with the headmistress's daughter."

"What?" I asked.

Alison shook her head. "You didn't know? Hello! Georgia *Drake*."

"*Georgia* is Headmistress Drake's *daughter*?! I had no idea," I said.

Alison grinned. "That's nothing new, Silver. See ya."

I gave her a half wave as I started up the sidewalk to Winchester, but my mind was preoccupied. If the Belles really had found a way to hack into my e-mail, I wondered if it could have had anything to do with the fact that one of them was the headmistress's daughter. I

still wasn't sure how Georgia could have pulled it off—
but either way, no more gut-spilling e-mails for me. If
I had something big to say—to anyone—it would have
to happen live and in person.

15

PASMINE?

I NERVOUSLY APPLIED A COAT OF LIP GLOSS— chocolate raspberry—and stepped out of the bathroom. In a minute I had to leave for film class. If I didn't love the class so much, I would have requested to drop it by now.

I grabbed my film book, tucked it under my arm, and headed for the common room. Paige had been there for a couple of hours testing a new recipe. Maybe if I begged and gave her the sad-eyes and trembling-lip combo, she'd let me taste something yummy.

Laughter came from inside—Paige was probably fending off our floor mates Annabella and Suichin. They always tried to sneak bites of Paige's delicious food too.

"Hey," I called, walking around the corner. "What are you guys do—" I stopped in the doorway.

Paige and Jasmine sat together on the couch, facing each other and grinning. A fire warmed the room, and the smell of hot apple cider wafted through the air. They both looked cozy in pajama pants and hoodies.

"Paaaige?" My voice was high and weird.

Paige's head whipped in my direction and she almost spilled her drink. "Sasha, hey." She uncurled her legs and put her feet on the floor.

"Wanna sit?" Jas asked, patting the couch cushion. She'd obviously recovered from her soda bath just hours ago.

"No, thanks," I said. I couldn't believe it. All this time, I thought Paige had been cooking, and she'd actually been chatting with Jasmine!

"I was baking and Jas came in for a snack," Paige explained. "We've been discussing Troy's hotness factor."

I shrugged. "You guys have fun. I've got film."

"Sash," Paige said. She got up.

But I mumbled, "Gotta go," and walked out of the room, leaving Winchester behind. *Calm down*, I told myself. Paige just felt bad for Jasmine—especially after the soda thing. Paige was the Polite Princess of Winchester. She was probably just trying to be nice.

I walked into the brightly lit media center and weaved

through the students waiting in line for popcorn, candy, or soda. Inside the theater I took my seat and rubbed my temple.

Jacob sat next to me and dropped his book bag on the ground. He turned and looked at me.

"Is something . . . wrong?" he asked.

I shifted to glance at him.

"I mean, I know you're mad at me. And you should be. I'm not talking about that." He brushed his hair out of his eye.

"Then what?" I asked, shrugging.

Jacob took another deep breath. "I don't know. There's just something. And if it *is* just because of Callie and me, I'm really sorry."

My shoulders slumped. I wasn't ready to forgive him, but Jacob was definitely trying. I looked at him for a second and saw that his green eyes were full of concern. For a moment, I saw the Jacob that I used to like—the Zac Efron look-alike who'd given me extra marshmallows at the Sweet Shoppe that one time. The one who'd made a horse movie for me because he knew how much I loved horses.

"Nothing else is wrong," I whispered.

Mr. Ramirez walked into the room, saving me from having to say anything else.

But I could feel Jacob searching my face as if he was looking for a clue. I pretended to be paying attention as Mr. Ramirez started class, but all I could think about was how much longer I'd have to keep Eric a secret.

16

WHEN BORED,
GO RIDING!

IT WAS ONLY ELEVEN A.M. AND I'D ALREADY
crossed everything off my Sunday to-do list: I'd spoken
to my parents (skipping over the part, of course, where I
have a secret boyfriend—but filling them in plenty about
my good grades), finished my math homework, and read
the first two chapters for English.

But now Paige and I were antsy to do something fun.

"Movie?" Paige asked. She sat up at the end of her bed,
looking hopefully at me.

"Nah," I said, spinning around in my desk chair.
"Magazines?"

"Read all the good ones. TV?"

I shook my head. "Nothing on."

We both sighed. Our room felt tiny today. Bleak

sunlight came through the window between our beds. I tried not to notice how messy my desk was compared to Paige's. Mine was covered with stacks of homework papers, graded tests, and old issues of *Horse Illustrated*.

"We could . . ." I paused. "Omigod! We should go on a trail ride!"

Paige grinned. "With me? Riding?"

"Yes! Eric could come too, and we'd have lots of fun."

"Will Mr. Conner let me? You know I've never ridden before."

I thought for a second. "Well, Eric and I could promise to give you a riding lesson before we go. Mr. Conner trusts us. He'll say yes."

Paige hopped off her bed. "Okay! Then yes! I'm going *riding*."

I texted Eric. *Want 2 trail ride w/ P & me?*

My phone buzzed right away.

"He's in," I said. "Let's get dressed."

I tossed a pair of breeches to Paige.

"Thanks," she said.

We paired them with heavy sweaters and pulled our hair into low ponytails. I swiped on pineapple gloss and put on my riding boots.

"Can I wear these?" Paige asked. She held up her wedge boots.

"No way," I said. "Here." I gave her a spare pair of riding boots. "If you fell off in those boots, your foot could get caught in the stirrup. The horse could drag you."

Paige swallowed.

"But that's not going to happen!" I said quickly. "Eric and I will help you. Don't worry."

Paige gave me a small smile. "Please. I'm not worried. You're Miss Superstar Rider of Canterwood."

I shook my head, laughing.

Paige moved in front of our full-length mirror and checked her reflection.

"I should totally buy riding clothes," she said. "They're so chic."

I grabbed my camera, snapping a pic of her. "There. Now you'll have future fashion inspiration."

Paige nodded. "And I'll totally e-mail that pic to my parents *after* we're done. Otherwise, my mom'll find some magic way to stop us."

At the stable, we went straight to Mr. Conner's office. I knocked on his door.

"Come in," he called.

Paige and I walked into the office and he smiled at us.

He'd met Paige last fall when I introduced her to Charm.

Mr. Conner was sitting behind his giant wooden desk, in front of a pile of paperwork. His spacious office was huge and my eyes wandered to the blue championship ribbons on the wall behind him. I wanted a wall of blues just like those.

"What can I do for you girls?" Mr. Conner asked.

"Well," I started, "I was wondering if Eric and I could take Paige on a short trail ride. We'd take the easiest trail. And walking and trotting only. Promise."

"A trail ride, huh? Have you ridden before?" Mr. Conner asked Paige.

She shook her head. "No. But I think Sasha could teach me."

"Eric and I would give her a lesson first," I said. "And we'd put her on a superquiet horse."

Mr. Conner drummed his fingers on the desk, then looked up at us. "I want to watch Paige ride before you go. If she's comfortable and I think it's safe, it's fine with me."

"Thank you!" Paige and I said in unison.

"Get Chomp for her," Mr. Conner said.

We thanked him again and left.

"Yes!" Paige said when we got in the aisle. "Is Chomp a good horse?"

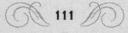

"Oh, yeah," I said. "He's supercalm and sweet. You'll love him."

"Where'd he get his name?"

"Uh, well," I said, pausing. "It's rumored that he bites riders he doesn't like."

Paige stopped. "*Bites*?! Sasha!"

"It's not true! Really," I said. "People made it up. Or Mr. Conner would never let you ride him. Swear."

Paige eyed me, but followed me to the tack room. We grabbed Chomp's tack and grooming kit and headed for his stall.

"There's Eric," Paige said, pointing down to Luna's stall.

We waved and he walked over to us. "Hey," he said, looking at Paige. "Ready for your first ride?"

Paige crossed her fingers. "I think so!"

"We have to give Paige a lesson first," I said. "Mr. C will watch her ride, and when she totally impresses him, we can go."

Eric nodded. "I'll groom Luna and Charm, so you can give Paige her lesson."

"You sure?" I asked.

"No prob," Eric said.

I smiled. "Thanks, Eric." I felt my cheeks grow warm

when I realized I'd been staring at him maybe a little too long.

But Eric didn't seem to notice. He just started for the tack room, and Paige and I went to Chomp's stall.

"He really likes you," Paige whispered.

"I hope so," I said. "Because I *really* like him."

"You *have* to be dying that you haven't gone on a date yet."

I nodded, coiling the lead line around my hand. "I am. But I'm just not ready for everyone to know."

I took Chomp from his stall, and Paige helped me lead him to an empty set of crossties. Paige eyed him warily, staying out of biting range, but Chomp didn't even blink at her.

"If he bites me," Paige said, "you owe me a trip to the Sweet Shoppe."

"Deal. But see?" I said, patting his neck. "He's totally fine."

"At least I know how to groom this time," Paige said. She picked up a body brush.

"Wait till you learn how to tack up."

We groomed Chomp, then I brought over the saddle pad.

"Okay," I said. "We put on the saddle pad to prevent

the saddle from rubbing sores into the horse's back."

Paige nodded. "Got it."

I picked up the English saddle, heaved it into the air, and placed it gently on Chomp's back. "You reach under and grab the girth, then tighten it to keep the saddle in place."

Paige watched. "Does it hurt?"

"It's not supposed to," I said. "You take your time so you don't pinch the horse."

I tightened Chomp's girth and moved to his head. "Grab the bridle, please," I told Paige, pointing to it.

She handed it to me.

"So, you put the reins over the horse's head and take off the halter," I said. "Now we put on the bridle."

Paige stepped closer to see. I could do this in my sleep, so I had to think about how to explain it to her.

"You hold the crown piece with your right hand and the bit with your left. Put the bit right under the horse's mouth and say, 'Open.'"

"Crown piece, bit, open," Paige repeated.

"Open," I told Chomp. He opened his mouth and I slid the bit inside while pulling the crown piece over his ears. "There. Now, we make sure nothing's twisted or too tight and we're ready!"

"Wow," Paige said. "I had no idea it was so complicated! You have to remember all of that."

"It's easy now. You'd remember it after a few times too. C'mon. You need a helmet."

We led Chomp to the tack room and I held him in the aisle while Paige found a helmet. She put it on, pieces of pretty strawberry-gold hair peeking out, and we walked into the arena.

"This place is huge," Paige marveled, playing with the silver ring on her thumb.

"Don't worry. I won't let go of the reins till you're ready," I promised.

"'Kay." Paige took a deep breath.

I motioned for her to stand next to Chomp.

"Grab onto his mane up here," I patted the spot. "And put your left foot in the stirrup. Kind of bounce, then push yourself up into the saddle."

"You'll hold him, right?" Paige's eyes widened as she looked at the saddle.

"Swear. He won't move."

Paige hesitated for a second before she grabbed Chomp's black mane and stuck her foot in the stirrup. She hopped twice, then lifted herself into the saddle.

"Excellent!" I said. "That was perfect."

Keeping a hand on the reins, I moved to Chomp's head. "Put the stirrups on the balls of your feet and push your heels down."

Paige did. "Like that?"

"Yep. And hold the reins like this." I stepped back by Chomp's neck and rearranged Paige's fingers on the reins.

"How do I make him go where I want?" Paige asked, looking down at me.

"You gently pull the rein in the direction you want to go. If you want him to speed up, tap him with your heels. To slow, just pull back gently on the reins."

"That's a lot!"

"It is, but it'll just come to you. It's weird. But you'll see."

Paige nodded, clutching the reins. Her wide eyes peeked out from under the brim of her helmet. I swear I could see her heart beating through her sweater.

"Let's walk. Squeeze gently with your legs," I told Paige.

She did and Chomp walked forward. I kept my hands on the reins and helped guide him in a circle.

The scared look on Paige's face started to fade after several laps. "This is fun!" she said finally. "I'm actually riding!"

I smiled. "You totally are! Say, 'Whoa,' and pull on the reins."

"Whoa," Paige said.

Chomp slowed to a stop and I patted his neck. "Start again."

Paige urged Chomp forward, smiling when he responded. "He's listening!"

"He better," I joked. "He's got Paige Parker on board!"

I guided Chomp around the arena a few more times.

"I'm going to let you go," I said, releasing the reins.

Paige's shoulders stiffened. "Um, okay."

"Relax," I soothed. "I'm right here. You've got it."

Paige squeezed Chomp with her legs. The bay ambled forward a few steps and stopped, looking back at me.

"More leg pressure," I said. "Tap him with your heels and squeeze with your legs. Tell him to walk."

"Walk," Paige commanded, her voice firm. Chomp walked forward—right to the wall! He stopped with his face to the wall, and flicked his tail.

"Sasha," Paige said in a tiny voice. "I did it wrong."

I tried not to laugh. "No, you didn't. I'm coming!"

I grabbed Chomp's reins and led him away from the wall. "Try it again," I told Paige.

She got Chomp to walk forward, and this time, they made several successful circuits around the arena.

"Looking good," Mr. Conner called, walking over to me.

I crossed my fingers and willed Paige to ride well and not run Chomp into the wall. Out of the corner of my eye, I watched Mr. Conner looking at Paige. She made a few laps around the arena and I knew she'd nailed it.

"You taught her well," he said.

"Thanks," I said, fighting back a grin. "So . . . can we go?"

He nodded. "Just stick to the designated trails and don't go off exploring. No cross-country, either."

"Okay, we won't."

"Nice work, Paige. Have fun," Mr. Conner said as he left.

Paige smiled and guided Chomp over to me. "I passed!"

"Um, of course. *I* taught you."

Paige rolled her eyes. "Let's go."

Eric, Paige, and I rode the horses side by side across the stable yard. Paige was in the middle—the safest spot for a new rider. I took a breath of fresh spring air and tipped my face toward the sun. It felt good to be out on the trails.

"You okay?" I asked her.

"Yup," she said, smiling. "Fine."

I leaned forward to rub Charm's neck. But when I looked up, my mood dimmed. Callie stood yards away, watching us. Her eyes landed on Paige, and shock registered on her face. Before the Jacob mess, Callie and I had planned to take Paige on a trail ride.

I slumped into Charm's saddle and couldn't stop looking at Callie, who looked like she was going to cry. She started to wave at us, but her hand fell limply into the air.

I tore my eyes away from Callie, not looking at her as we rode by. We kept the horses at a walk as we started toward the woods. Paige and Eric didn't say anything about Callie, and I didn't bring it up.

"Like it?" I asked Paige.

"Love. It." She patted Chomp's neck. "It's a totally new perspective from up here. Trail riding rocks."

"I could ride out here every day," Eric said. "And Luna would love it."

"Yeah, Charm wouldn't mind if we never had another lesson," I said. "He'd be supercool with hanging out in the pasture and relaxing on the trails."

The three of us chatted easily, and soon I'd forgotten all about Callie.

17

TO SNITCH OR NOT TO SNITCH

"SO WILL YOUR MOM FREAK WHEN YOU TELL her that you went riding?" Eric asked.

Paige nodded. "Oh, yeah. She doesn't think riding is a 'ladylike' activity. Now, if the horses had pulled us in a carriage, she'd love it."

We laughed and I looked around, taking in the scenery. The dirt trail, worn by the hooves of many horses, twisted through the forest. Bare trees flanked both sides of the trail and cast strange shadows over us. I glanced over at Eric and saw that he was already staring at me. We smiled at each other. I didn't look away until Charm snorted and pulled on the reins.

"This is gorgeous," Paige said. She looked like an expert equestrian now, easily guiding Chomp down the path.

We'd reached the part of the trail that was separated from a large open field by a stone wall.

"It's my favorite," I said.

We edged the horses closer to the wall. Charm tossed his head and strained against the reins, begging me to let him go faster.

"Want to trot?" Eric asked with a nod to Charm.

I looked over at Paige. "You can handle it," I said. "And we'll walk whenever you want."

"Okay. How do I trot?"

"Touch him with your heels and say, 'Trot,'" I instructed.

I moved Charm closer to Paige, ready to help her if necessary.

"Trot," Paige said. She tapped her boots against Chomp's sides. Eric and I did the same to Luna and Charm. All three horses started trotting at the same time.

"Good job," I told Paige.

Paige's head bobbed as she bounced in the saddle. Her hands jerked up and down, and she almost lost a stirrup.

"Try to post," Eric said, pulling Luna beside Chomp. He showed Paige how to move in the saddle.

Paige, her tongue sticking out of the corner of her

mouth, stood up straight in the saddle, then plopped back down. "That's not right, is it?" she asked.

"Move forward and backward instead of up and down," I said. "Like this."

Paige watched for a few seconds before trying it again. After a few more tries, her posting finally resembled, well, posting.

"There!" I said. "You got it."

We let the horses trot for several yards.

Paige pointed to the far side of the field. "Someone's riding over there."

I half stood in the stirrups and squinted to see. A gray blur raced over the grass and leaped the stone wall. The rider, pumping her arms, urged the horse to a near gallop and they hurtled toward a line of brush hedges.

"Oh, my God," I said. "It's Jasmine and Phoenix."

I looked over at Eric. His fingers clenched around the reins. His face reddened. "I can't believe she'd do something so stupid like riding alone—especially so recklessly," he said. "She could hurt herself—not to mention Phoenix."

"Isn't she experienced enough to ride by herself?" Paige asked.

"It's never safe to jump alone. Especially not like that," I said.

Paige nodded. "But maybe she asked someone to come

with her and they said no." Eric and I exchanged a look. We knew better. Jasmine wanted to ride alone.

We started our horses across the field. Jasmine didn't slow Phoenix as she jumped him over six hedges. She turned Phoenix in our direction and her head snapped up.

Jasmine kicked Phoenix forward and he galloped toward us. His speed increased with every stride. He looked like molten steel coming at us.

Jasmine let Phoenix gallop until he was just yards away. She pulled him to a halt, his hooves digging into the grass.

"Spying on me?" Jasmine huffed. "Really?" She dropped Phoenix's knotted reins around his neck and crossed her arms.

"Riding alone?" I mimicked. "Really?"

Jasmine rolled her eyes. "So what? Like I want all of *you* stealing my technique."

Eric laughed. He urged Luna forward, stopping her next to Phoenix. He glared at Jasmine and she seemed to sink into the saddle. "We take lessons together. I see you ride every day."

Jasmine's mouth flopped open for a second. "Whatever, *Eric*."

I shrugged. "Mr. Conner will flip when I tell him what you've been doing."

Jasmine adjusted the collar of her red and black tartan coat. "You're going to snitch on me for *this*?"

"Risking a horse is kind of a big deal," I replied.

I could tell that Eric was furious at Jas for putting Phoenix in danger. His jaw was set, his gaze was intense, and he was obviously trying to keep his mouth shut. He'd been staring Jasmine down since she'd ridden over to us. He truly cared about horses, and it made me like him even more.

"So?" Jas asked. "Are you going to tell, or what?"

Eric's eyes stayed on her.

"Ride back with us now," I said.

"And promise never do it again," Eric added.

"Or," I said, "we'll have no other choice but to tell Mr. Conner."

Jasmine stared at me for a looong time. Her face turned pink and she mashed her lips together.

"Fine," she spat.

"Good," Eric said lightly. "Let's go." He motioned for Jas to ride in front of him. She rolled her eyes and followed Paige and me out of the field. We got back on the trail, no one saying a word.

Jasmine, shoving Phoenix between Charm and Chomp, rode next to me.

"Did you drag Paige out here just so you could have an actual friend to ride with?" Jasmine asked me. "Someone other than Intermediate Eric?"

"FYI, Paige wanted to come," I said. "And stop trashing Eric about being an intermediate. *You* are too!"

Jasmine laughed. "Please. You're one to talk. Luck got you where you are—nothing else."

"Sasha's a great rider," Eric said. "Way better than you'll ever be, and you know it."

"Ooooh," Jasmine cooed. "How sweet. What? Is she your girlfriend or something?"

I ducked my head and shifted my eyes to Eric. I wanted to tell Jasmine the truth, but I couldn't. Jasmine would tell everyone. Eric just looked at me, like he was waiting for me to say something.

"He's being a good friend," Paige interrupted, saving me. "I'd thought you knew something about that when we talked in the common room. Guess not."

Jasmine stared straight ahead, not even bothering to comment back. We were all silent for the rest of the ride.

Back at the stable, we crosstied our horses and groomed them. Heather, Julia, and Alison walked by Jasmine without

saying a word. They were obviously afraid of Violet, not that they'd ever admit it.

Mr. Conner walked up to us, stopping in front of Paige.

"Did you have a good ride?" he asked.

"It was great," Paige said. "Thanks for letting me ride."

Mr. Conner smiled. "You're welcome. Anytime." He walked toward Jasmine and she hurriedly went back to grooming.

"Jasmine," Mr. Conner said. "I scheduled your advanced team testing for next Saturday. If you need any advice or help preparing, let me know."

"Okay, thanks." Jasmine said. "I'll be ready,"

I groaned. Days when riding lessons were fun? Almost over.

As Mr. Conner walked away, Jasmine peered at me from down the aisle and grinned. "Guess who's about to become your new teammate?"

Groan. I flicked the dandy brush over Charm's back, working hard not to think about how everything was about to change. And definitely not for the better.

18

DEFINE "SPORT"

IGNORING CALLIE DURING ENGLISH CLASS had almost become an art. I bent over my Tuesday to-do list and didn't look at her as she took her seat.

"Umm, so . . ." Callie started. I looked at her for a second before scribbling fake notes on my paper. *Sparkles. Charm. Eric.* "How's bio? One of my friends in the class said Peterson has been giving lots of quizzes."

I shrugged without looking up.

Mr. Davidson walked into the room, shutting the door behind him. "Pop quiz time, everyone! Please get out a clean sheet of paper and clear your desk.

"Question one," Mr. Davidson started.

I looked down at my paper, trying to remember

everything I'd read last night in Sir Arthur Conan Doyle's *The Hound of the Baskervilles*. Well, more like *tried* to read while I shopped at Express online. I'd needed—okay, wanted—a new skirt for my future first date with Eric. The date I could go on the second I told people about us. I hadn't found anything perfect enough, but it had taken me hours to discover that.

"What year did Doyle write *The Hound of the Baskervilles*?" Mr. Davidson asked.

I stared at my page. *Think!*

I scribbled, *1901*. That sounded right . . . didn't it?

"Question two," Mr. Davidson said. He glanced at his question sheet. "Who narrated the book?"

Holmes? Or Watson. Holmes. No. That sounded too obvious. I stared at my paper. Online shopping had *so* been the wrong choice last night!

Mr. Davidson stepped out from behind his desk. "Question three."

Wait! I still hadn't answered the second question. I wrote down *Holmes*, then erased it and put *Watson.*

A sick feeling crept into my stomach. One quiz wouldn't kill me—I had an A in the class—but after a rocky fall semester, I didn't want to fail anything.

Mr. Davidson asked three more questions, and with

each one, I got more confused. I had some serious work to do tonight.

I hurried down the stable aisle to the tack room. *Only a few more lessons without Jasmine*, I thought.

I pushed open the door and walked right into a Jasbashing session courtesy of the Trio.

"She's beyond pathetic," Heather said. She was sitting in a folding chair. Julia and Alison were cross-legged on horse blankets in front of her. "She really thinks that teaming up with the Belles will save her?"

Alison shook her head. "Please. They'll use her and kick her out of their group so fast. She'll *never* be their real friend."

"I'd watch it," I said, grabbing Charm's tack. "Violet seemed pretty serious when she said that stuff to you, Heather."

"So what?" Julia asked. "It's not like they can do anything to us."

Heather looked over, daring me to disagree. "Seriously, Silver. I just *let* Violet think she won that day. Like *I* listen to anyone."

Julia and Alison nodded.

Whatever. Their funeral. I shrugged and slipped out the door.

After my lesson I walked and groomed Charm. I turned him loose in his stall and went to the grain room for his feed.

I finished measuring Charm's grain and took it to his stall. "Here, boy," I said. I hung up his bucket, then kissed his cheek. "See you tomorrow!"

I dashed to the stable exit and found Eric waiting for me.

"Haven't seen you in a while," I said.

"I know," he said seriously. "And I have a dorm meeting in Blackwell in a few minutes. But IM tonight?"

I couldn't believe I was about to say it, but . . .

"I can't," I said, scuffing my boots as we walked. "I want to, but I messed up in English today. I'm not studying enough and I can't let my grades slip."

"Yeah, you can't mess up your shot at the YENT," Eric agreed. "No problem—we'll talk later."

"But if you happen to text me once or twice," I said, looking at him sideways, "I think I can take a little break for that."

He laughed. "Deal."

We turned down the sidewalk that led to Winchester.

"I forgot to tell you that I had the easiest lesson *ever* today," I said. "Mr. Conner must have been distracted or something, 'cause he barely made us do anything."

Eric smirked. "I'll tell him you said that."

"Oh, please. And then I'll tell him that you looove riding without stirrups."

"You wouldn't!"

"I totally would. And you're secretly relieved that my lesson was easy. You were afraid you'd have to carry me back to Winchester if I'd had another grueling class."

Eric sighed. "Yeah, Sash. Carrying you would be so hard." He wiped his forehead.

I swatted his arm. "Stop it!"

We both laughed. All of a sudden, I really wanted to hold his hand. Maybe I could and no one would notice. I started to inch my hand toward his, while trying to act cool. My fingers almost touched his and—oops.

Jacob was walking down the sidewalk right toward us.

I jerked my fingers away from Eric. That had been too close!

Jacob, Eric, and I stopped, and the guys eyed each other.

"'Sup," Jacob said, nodding at Eric.

"Hi," I said.

Eric remained silent. Awkward.

Jacob, shifting from one black Converse to the other,

smiled at us. But I knew Jacob—it was his fake smile.

Jacob eyed our boots. "Done riding?"

"Yeah," I said. "I just finished a lesson and Eric was grooming his horse."

I stared at the sidewalk, trying to think of something—anything—else to say. But I couldn't come up with one thing.

Jacob looked at Eric. "So, you play any sports?"

Random, much?

"I *ride*," Eric said, like, *hello*?

"I know," Jacob said. "But I mean *sports*."

Ohhhh, Jacob.

"Riding *is* a sport," Eric said.

Jacob shrugged. "*Well*—"

"Not 'well,'" Eric said, his voice sharp. "Riding's a sport. You ever jumped a horse? Or galloped one across a field? You have to be pretty strong to pull that off."

I wanted to jump in, but my mind was still totally, utterly blank.

"But basically, it's just sitting and telling the horse where to go," Jacob said.

Oh, no, he didn't!!

"Wait a second!" I yelled. "Are you kidding me?! You know how hard I work at riding. It's nothing like that!"

Eric leaned toward Jacob. "Just walk away, man."

"What's your problem?" Jacob asked.

"*You're* my problem. You think you can treat Sasha like you did and everything's okay?"

The boys glared at each other.

I didn't want to be in the middle of this! What should I say?! I just stood there not knowing what to do.

Jacob ducked his head a little. "Look," he said to me. "I shouldn't have—"

Eric stared at Jacob. "You shouldn't have done a lot of things."

"Guys," I said. "C'mon."

Eric glared at Jacob for a few more seconds.

"Seriously," I said. "Stop it. I'm going back to Winchester."

"Fine. I'll walk you," Eric said.

We split up to walk around Jacob, then started down the sidewalk together.

"Sorry," Eric said. "But he's a jerk. He was lucky to have even gotten one chance with you and he blew it." He unclenched his hands.

"Thanks for standing up for me," I said. "Jacob is . . . I don't know why he was being like that."

Eric shrugged. "He doesn't deserve you. He never did."

As we walked back to Winchester, I tried to imagine why Jacob had been so weird with Eric. What did he care anymore anyway? He had Callie. Didn't he? But by the time I said good night to Eric, I still had nothing.

I pulled open the dorm door—I needed to find Paige ASAP. Our midweek cookie break was about to happen a day early. After I'd witnessed that round between Jacob and Eric, this was a cookie emergency.

19

PLUS ONE

"I CAN'T BELIEVE *TEEN CUISINE* PREMIERES soon," I said to Paige. It was a lazy Saturday afternoon and we were sprawled on our beds.

"One month," Paige said. "I'm so nervous!"

"Why? I know you did great!"

"You don't know that. What if I'm awful? Everyone will see it. In HD!" Paige sat up and pulled her lavender pillow across her lap.

"You were NOT awful—I know it. The show will be great. And . . . I've been thinking that we need to celebrate when it airs."

I hopped off my bed and pulled on my boots. Jasmine's testing was today and I wanted to go to the stable and see what—if anything—had happened. I had no doubt the Trio was already there.

Paige's expression brightened. "Celebrate? Like how?"

"Oh, I don't know," I said slowly. "I had this idea that you'll *totally* hate, but I guess I'll tell you."

"Sasha! Spill!"

I grinned. "I think we need to throw a premiere party!"

Paige fell backward onto her bed. "Yeeesss! That's perfect!"

I grabbed a notebook and scribbled the ideas I'd been thinking about for a couple of days.

"We'll throw it in the media center," I said. "We can have a red carpet, drinks, and food. We'll all dress up and everyone can watch the show together."

"Oooh! We can get our guy friends to be security," Paige said, giggling. "We'll dress them up in uniforms."

"Yeah! And we can all watch it on the big plasma screen."

Paige leaned over and grabbed a notepad from her bedside table. "I'll start making a VIP guest list and I'll reserve the room."

"Get the biggest room," I said. "You're gonna have lots of fans."

Paige's eyes widened. "Fans? No way."

"They'll love you and the show," I said. "Promise. I've got to go, but we'll plan more later?"

"'Kay," Paige said. "I hope Jas falls off."

"Paige!" I said, feigning shock. "I can't believe you just said that!"

"Well," Paige said quickly. "Not enough to hurt her or anything."

I nodded. "Suuure."

When I got to the stable, I texted Eric. @ *Jas's tsting. Bleh.*

Eric wrote me back. :(*mayb she'll mess up.*

But we both knew she wouldn't. Jasmine was going to rock the testing.

Callie and the Trio trickled into the skybox. We all grabbed front-row seats.

"We know she's going to make it, right?" Julia asked. She popped a piece of neon green gum into her mouth.

"Yep," I said. Everyone else nodded.

Jasmine entered the arena, mounted Phoenix, and rode him into the center. She looked up at us and waved pageant-queen-style.

"Oh, puh-leeze," Heather said, rolling her eyes.

Mr. Conner walked inside. He nodded to us before turning to Jasmine. "Would you like to have a private testing?" he asked.

She shook her head. "No, I don't mind if they watch. They might be my teammates after this!"

Eww.

"You all must remain silent," Mr. Conner reminded us. "If you say a word, you're out."

We nodded. Heather, clasping her hands, leaned forward on the edge of her chair. This was the last thing she—or any of us—wanted.

"Go ahead and warm Phoenix up," Mr. Conner said.

Jasmine took Phoenix around the arena at a walk, trot, and canter until Mr. Conner signaled her to stop.

"Let's get started," Mr. Conner said. "You'll take Phoenix through several exercises. Just listen to my commands and do them as soon as you can after I ask. Understand?"

"Yes, sir," Jasmine said. She narrowed her eyes, staring between Phoenix's ears.

Her face gave away nothing. She was totally determined to make the team. She sat up straight in the saddle, pushed down her heels, and rested her hands over Phoenix's neck.

Game. On.

"Head out to the rail and do a sitting trot," Mr. Conner commanded.

Jasmine sat to Phoenix's trot. They moved around the arena, looking perfect together.

"Halt," Mr. Conner called.

Within seconds, Jasmine brought Phoenix to a smooth stop. He stood, not moving, while he waited for Jasmine to give him another signal.

"Reverse direction and posting trot," Mr. Conner said.

Jasmine turned Phoenix, then got him trotting in a few strides. She took him around the arena twice. Mr. Conner marked a few things on his clipboard before he looked up.

"Halt and back up," Mr. Conner instructed.

Jasmine stopped Phoenix and asked him to back. He tucked his chin, taking quick steps backward.

"Good," Mr. Conner said.

He took Jasmine through a few more exercises before holding up his hand.

Jasmine, slowing Phoenix, was barely able to hide her grin. She knew the spot on the advanced team was almost hers.

"Let's move to jumping," Mr. Conner said. "Mike and Doug have arranged six jumps at the end of the arena. Take them once. After that we'll discuss your ride."

"Okay," Jasmine said, nodding. She shoved her heels down and tightened the reins.

"Bets?" Alison whispered.

"Zero faults," Callie said under her breath.

The rest of us nodded. There was no way she'd miss a jump. I scooted forward so I could see every inch of the arena.

She circled Phoenix twice before heeling him toward the first yellow and blue vertical. Phoenix jumped over the poles, swishing his tail with pride when he landed cleanly. Jasmine yanked on his mouth, checking him, and then urging him over two faux-brush jumps.

I looked at Mr. Conner—he was *maaad*. He crossed his arms, shaking his head. He'd told Jas a zillion times not to be rough on Phoenix, but she kept doing it.

Everything else about her ride was amazing (sigh), but her forcefulness with Phoenix was hard to watch. I hurt for Phoenix when she jabbed him with her heels. But Phoenix, a well-trained pro, listened to all of Jasmine's commands. She got him over two double oxers and kicked him a stride before the final, and highest, vertical.

Phoenix launched into the air but clipped the rail with his back hoof. It wobbled in the holder and thudded to the ground behind them. Jasmine tugged Phoenix to a halt in front of Mr. Conner.

"Can I do it again?" she asked. "I don't know why he did that."

"No need to go again," Mr. Conner said. "I saw enough to evaluate you."

Jasmine pouted. Then she seemed to remember that Mr. Conner was still watching her. She fake smiled and patted Phoenix while Mr. Conner flicked through his paperwork.

"I'm not going to make you wait for my decision," Mr. Conner said a few minutes later. "You've already tested later than everyone else, so that wouldn't be fair."

The Trio, Callie, and I glanced at one another. That *was* unfair—to *us!* Mr. Conner had made us wait *forever* for his decision.

"Would you like the other girls to leave before we speak?" Mr. Conner asked.

Jasmine shook her head. "They can stay." She sniffed. "I'll need support if I didn't do well."

Oh, vomit.

"All right, then. Let me get to the point. Your flatwork

was sharp," Mr. Conner said. "Your timing was impeccable and you have a deep seat. Without a doubt, you're a talented rider."

Jasmine beamed.

Mr. Conner took a breath. "However, you still muscle Phoenix around. There's simply no reason for that. You're skilled enough that even the slightest cues to him will be sufficient. You cannot continue to force Phoenix through every riding session."

Jasmine's happy face disappeared. "Okay," she whispered.

Mr. Conner consulted his clipboard. "Unfortunately, that's why I cannot grant you a spot on the advanced team. If you had listened to my advice and had not forced Phoenix around the jumps, I would have given you a seat."

Beside me, Callie gasped. I looked back at the Trio— they were all grinning. We'd all been sure that Jas would make it.

I stared down at Jasmine. Her cheeks and nose were pink as if she was swallowing back tears. I wished she had a friend waiting for her when she went back to her room.

Mr. Conner looked up at Jasmine. "To be part of the team, you must be willing to take direction and agree to work much harder on softening your directions to Phoenix."

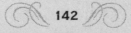

Jasmine just nodded.

Mr. Conner looked up at her. "I look forward to watching you test again in the fall. If you follow directions then, I'm sure you'll make the team."

Breath whooshed out of everyone in the skybox. I don't think any of us could believe it—the old team was still intact!

Jasmine didn't look at us as she dismounted and led Phoenix out of the arena. She'd been sure she was going to make it and she'd let everyone know it. She'd been humiliated. Again. It was an endless string of embarrassments for Jasmine.

Callie, the Trio, and I stood and left the skybox.

Julia high-fived Heather and grinned at all of us. "Jas totally deserved not to make it," Julia said. "Now she's back on the loser team."

"It's not a loser team," I snapped.

Alison looked at me. "Why do *you* care?"

I shrugged. I shouldn't have said anything, but I wasn't going to let them trash Eric's team. "I don't. Whatever."

I walked away from them and went to Charm's stall. I let myself inside and hugged his neck.

"Jas didn't make it, boy," I said. "Our team is safe for a little while longer." But it didn't make me feel particularly happy to say it. No matter how awful she was, Jas *did* work hard at riding. She deserved to make the advanced team, but she had to start treating Phoenix better—and listening to Mr. Conner.

Someone knocked on the stall door. I looked up to see Callie.

"Hey," she said, her tone soft. "Can I come in?"

I shrugged. "Sure."

Callie let herself into the stall, stopping to pet Charm. "Sasha, I hate the way things are."

I tickled the tip of Charm's muzzle. The back-and-forth with Callie had been *so* exhausting. I didn't know how long I could stay mad at her for liking a guy—a guy I didn't even want anymore.

"Me too," I whispered.

Callie gave me a small smile. "I was completely wrong about the Jacob situation. I should have told you the second I started to like him. I never, ever meant for this to happen."

"I know you didn't." I sighed.

"But I was a *horrible* friend," Callie whispered. "I should have believed you the first time you told me about Eric. I'm so, so sorry."

I swallowed. This was the perfect opportunity to tell Callie that I was with Eric. But I was scared. Things with

Eric were so perfect, I didn't want to risk messing that up.

"Jacob's told me a million times how bad he feels," Callie added. "We both made a huge mistake."

I stared at her, not sure what to say. She pulled her dark brown wrap sweater tighter around her. She looked as miserable as I felt. I wanted to tell her that we should try being friends again, but I didn't.

We stood in silence for a few minutes. I ran my fingers through Charm's mane, pretending to search for knots, so I didn't have to look at Callie.

Finally, Callie sighed. She touched a fingertip to Charm's blaze. "I guess I'll go, then. But thanks for listening." She left the stall and I peeked over the door as she walked away.

Maybe things would never be the same, but then again . . . who knew what might happen next?

20

KARMA OR SOMETHING

HANGING OUT IN THE WINCHESTER COMMON room was one of my fave ways to spend a Sunday. And to-day my day was even better because, for once, I'd finished all of my homework early. Paige and I had made a run to the Sweet Shoppe for snacks. It was a gross gray day outside and we'd decided that we needed something with pink sprinkles—the cure to any blah day.

"I'm so excited about planning the premiere party," Paige said.

"Me too!"

We took our coconut cupcakes and hot chocolate over to the coffee table and sat facing each other on the ends of the couches that were closest to the warm fireplace.

"Livvie was here," I said, pointing to a green tea bag wrapper on the lamp table.

Paige nodded. "Only Livvie would drink that."

We sipped our hot chocolate and I took a bite of my cupcake. Mmm.

"I'm making a list of party food possibilities," Paige said. "I can't wait to start cooking and baking."

"And I can't wait to taste your new stuff," I said, grinning. "Let's talk decorations." I pulled out my sparkly purple notepad.

Paige leaned back on the couch. She played with one of her hoop earrings. "I've been thinking about that. Write down candles, a red carpet, a few posters to put on the walls . . ."

I scribbled on my pad. "Got it. And we'll just keep adding to the list as we think of stuff?"

"Good idea. I'm still working on the guest list."

I looked at my lap, then back at Paige. "Go ahead and invite Callie."

Paige's pen hovered above the paper. "Really?"

"She apologized again yesterday, and you know what? I believe her. And . . . I sort of miss her. I don't know . . . but maybe the fight's not worth it. I mean, I'm with Eric now. I really like him. And even though Callie and Jacob really hurt my feelings, it's not even like I *like* Jacob anymore. So invite her."

Paige reached over, touching my arm. "I'm so proud of you. You're a good person, Sasha Silver."

We both looked up when Jasmine walked into the common room. She wore simple black yoga pants and a burnt orange oversize sweater. I wished I didn't love her outfit so much.

"You're cold, Sasha," Jasmine said, shaking her head.

"What?" I asked.

Jasmine grabbed a root beer from the fridge, popped the top, and took a sip. "Well, even though Callie's your ex-BFF, you should still care that she's having a crisis."

"Omigod!" I stood up. "What's wrong?"

Jasmine sauntered over to the recliner by the fire, moving infuriatingly slow.

"Jasmine!" I snapped. "What?!"

She sighed. "Black Jack, or whatever his name is, got hurt. Callie's—"

Jasmine didn't even finish her sentence before I grabbed my coat and dashed out of the room. I shoved open the Winchester doors and ran all the way to the stable. I felt sick and like I couldn't catch my breath. *Please, please, don't let it be serious.* Callie would die if anything ever happened to Jack.

The arenas and stable yard were empty. I hurried through the stable entrance and ran down the main aisle, not caring if I got in trouble for running inside. Near the end of the aisle, I saw Callie and Mr. Conner standing by Jack. He was in crossties and Mr. O'Brady, the farrier, was bent over his right front hoof.

"Callie!" I called.

Callie turned to me, her eyes red and teary. I ran over to her and grabbed her in a hug.

"I-I hurt him," she sobbed, shaking against me.

"No, no," I soothed, squeezing her. "Whatever happened must have been an accident."

Mr. Conner, who had been murmuring something to Mr. O'Brady, turned to us.

"It *was* an accident," he said. "Callie, you did absolutely nothing wrong. These things do occur. It's *not* your fault."

"What happened?" I asked, looking at Callie.

She rubbed her face with her free hand. "We were jumping yesterday in the arena and Jack took a misstep. I pulled him up and checked him, but nothing felt wrong. We worked out in the arena for another half an hour and he never acted like he was in pain."

Callie took a shaky breath, composing herself.

"Today, we went through flatwork fine," she said. "I took him over *one* oxer and he limped." Callie struggled to hold back tears, which almost made me cry. "I should have called Mr. O'Brady yesterday!"

"You didn't know," I said. "You take the best care of Jack. The second you realized something was wrong, you got help."

Callie let out a shuddering breath. "I feel so bad for him."

Trying to stay out of Mr. O'Brady's way, we stepped by Jack's head. Callie rubbed his cheek and I patted his neck. The always calm Morab was obviously in pain—he rested the tip of his hoof on the ground and didn't even react when we touched him. His head drooped and his ears flicked dejectedly.

"You'll be okay, boy," I whispered.

Mr. O'Brady straightened and looked at us. He rubbed a hand over his bristly reddish beard. "I tested the hoof for soreness and it's definitely a bruise. It will heal, but he's going to need time."

Phew. A bruise was painful, but it could have been something much worse. Callie let out a breath, and her eyes brightened. "A bruise? Really?"

Mr. O'Brady nodded. "Yes. But you're not going to be

able to ride him for at least a week or two. In a few days, you can hand walk him over soft ground."

"Mike and Doug will help too," Mr. Conner assured Callie.

"You may also soak his hoof," Mr. O'Brady said. "But rest is what he really needs."

Mr. O'Brady gathered his tools and shook Mr. Conner's hand.

"Call me if his condition changes," Mr. O'Brady said. He patted Jack's neck.

Callie nodded. "We will. Thank you so much for helping him."

Mr. O'Brady left and we—Mr. Conner included—sighed with relief.

Mr. Conner turned to Callie. "Jack's going to be fine, Callie. We'll all help you with him, okay? Try not to worry."

"Thanks," Callie said. "I'll be here every second that I can to take care of him."

"And in the meantime, for practices," Mr. Conner said, "you're welcome to use any of the stable horses."

Callie glanced at Jack. "Thanks, but I'd feel bad riding when Jack's stuck in his stall."

I shook my head. "Cal, he's going to be sleeping and

healing. He won't know that you're riding another horse. Promise. You have to practice."

"Sasha's right," Mr. Conner said, picking up his clipboard from the table. "Come see me tomorrow afternoon. I'll help you find the right horse."

Callie paused for a second. "Okay. Thanks."

Mr. Conner patted Jack before walking back to his office.

"Let's take Jack back to his stall," I said.

Callie and I took a spot on either side of Jack's head. We unclipped the crossties and walked superslow down the aisle, letting Jack take his time. He limped down the aisle, bobbing his head with every step. Callie's eyes filled with tears as she led him. I couldn't even imagine how I would feel if this had happened to Charm. I took a deep breath, trying not to cry.

We finally got him to his stall and Callie released him inside. Jack, not even looking at Callie, moved into the corner by the hay net and put his head down.

"Oh, Jack," Callie said, her voice shaky.

"He's going to be fine," I said with empathy. "Promise."

I stood by Callie and we watched Jack for a few minutes. He didn't move, just kept still in the corner.

Callie was quiet for a minute. "Do you think it's, like, karma or something?"

"What?"

"I was going to ride him across the yard at midnight for the Belles' dare. Do you think this injury is payback because I almost did that to him?"

"No way," I said, shaking my head. "This was an accident. Stop blaming yourself. We're gonna heal him and you'll be riding him again soon enough. 'Kay?"

"Okay," Callie whispered.

"Have you had anything to eat today?" I asked. "You look sort of pale."

She shook her head. "No, but I don't want to leave him yet."

"If you want, I'll run to the Sweet Shoppe and grab us something. We can have a picnic by Jack's stall."

"Really?" Callie smiled and swiped at her eyes. "That would be great. Thanks."

"I'll be right back. Call me if you need something."

I left Callie with Jack and jogged all the way to the Sweet Shoppe—my second trip there today. The sky had darkened even more since Paige and I had been out. Extra pink sprinkles were absolutely necessary.

I texted Paige as I walked, knowing she was worried about Callie and Jack.

Jack will b fine. Bruised hoof. Needs rest.

Phew!! U staying w/ C? Paige texted.

4 a bit. B back ltr.

Inside the shop, I ordered hot chocolates, cookies, and minimuffins—all of the essential comfort foods. I moved away from the counter to wait for my order. The Trio sat at a corner table, sipping iced coffees. Their Burberry coats were draped over the backs of their chairs and they'd piled their gloves and scarves on a nearby table.

I walked over to them, noticing most of their table was covered with Julia's and Alison's history books, notepads, crumpled papers, and pens.

Heather eyed me. "What's wrong?" she asked warily. "You're making the damsel-in-distress face."

"Jack got hurt," I said.

Julia and Alison dropped their pens. "What?!" they asked in unison.

"What happened?" Heather asked.

"Callie jumped him yesterday and he landed weird," I said. "She checked him, thought he was fine, and kept riding. Today, she took him over an oxer and he started limping."

Heather's eyes were wide. "Did Mr. Conner call Mr. O'Brady?"

"Yeah, he just left. He said Jack bruised his hoof."

"That's awful," Julia said, shaking her head. "But it could have been much worse."

I nodded. "I know. Callie's still pretty upset, though. She's hanging with Jack while I get food."

"Poor Jack," Alison said.

The Trio was genuinely sorry. No matter what had happened among all of us, no one wanted to see a horse get hurt.

"We'll text her," Julia said, pulling out her phone.

Heather nodded. "Yeah, and we'll check on Jack whenever we're in the stable."

I nodded, thinking about how insane it was that the four of us were actually having a real conversation. For months Heather and I had done almost nothing but argue. But when it counted, she stepped up. And so did Julia and Alison. They'd be there for Callie while Jack healed.

"Thanks." I motioned to Julia and Alison's books. "How's the studying?"

The girls rolled their eyes.

"We're going to *die*," Julia said. "Mr. Fields is torturing us. We've got a giant history test coming up."

The barista called my name. "See you later," I said. "And good luck."

I walked away from the Trio and took my bag. Callie and I were finally going to sit down and talk. It was about time. Maybe while Jack healed his hoof, Callie and I could repair our friendship.

21

THE TALK

WHEN I GOT BACK TO THE STABLE, CALLIE had spread a clean blanket outside Jack's stall. She'd put up a webbed stall guard so we could sit in front of the door and see inside.

I settled onto the blanket, putting the bag between us. I pulled out the snacks and handed Callie her drink.

"Thanks," she said. "You picked all of my favorites."

I smiled.

We both picked up our chocolate chip muffins first and started to take tentative bites. *Tell her you want things to be okay,* I told myself. *It's the perfect time.*

"Callie," I said after a few minutes, "I'm so tired of being mad."

Callie stopped midbite and looked up at me. "You are?"

"Yeah. I hate this. I've been upset, but I miss you. We *all* messed up."

Callie shifted on the blanket and tucked her hair behind her ears. "*I* started it by not listening to you."

"Jack put things into perspective for me," I said. "For a long time, I wanted you to know how I felt when you wouldn't listen to me. But I'm done with that."

Callie put her face in her hands, then looked up at me. "I just wanted my friend back. I'm so glad you want me to be your friend again. And I owe you every detail about Jacob. All of it. If you want to hear it."

I nodded. I was ready.

Callie took a sip of her hot chocolate and held the cup with both hands. "I called Jacob the morning after the Sweetheart Soirée just to tell him that he needed to at least let you explain." Callie hesitated. "Jacob asked me if you really wanted to be with him or if you were crushing on Eric. I should have believed you when you said you were just friends and told that to Jacob. But I told him what I thought was the truth—I told him I thought you maybe liked Eric."

I just nodded. At the time I *had* been telling the truth—Eric and I really *had* been just friends. But now things were different—not that Callie knew that yet.

"I *never* should have said anything to Jacob about Eric," Callie said, curling her legs under her. "It was an awful thing to do."

"But you didn't lie on purpose. You really thought I liked Eric."

"Still. I shouldn't have said it. But that's how it started. We were both mad at you and that's how we . . . um, bonded. We both thought we'd lost you as a friend. Jacob wasn't ready to get over what happened at the dance, and I was sure you and Eric were together. Every time I saw you with Eric, it convinced me that I was right."

"I know it looked like I was with him," I said. And now I *was*. How would I ever be able to tell Callie that without making it seem like I'd *always* been crushing on Eric?

"And while Jacob was home on break and I was here," Callie continued, "we started texting and IMing. It just sort of happened. It totally freaked me out when I realized that I liked Jacob. That wasn't supposed to happen."

"You were always superfocused on school and riding," I said. "You must have liked Jacob a lot to take that step."

Callie put down her hot chocolate and ran her fingers through her hair. "I was so confused. I liked this guy, but I didn't know what to do. I didn't want to lose focus because of a boy."

I half smiled. "I kind of thought you'd be boyfriend-less till high school."

Callie laughed. "Me too!"

This was my chance to tell Callie that I was with Eric now. She was spilling her guts and I was sitting there not saying a word. But I'd *just* convinced her that I hadn't been with Eric. The truth could break us up before we even got our friendship started again.

"Thanks for telling me all of that," I said. "I never would have guessed it, but it does feel better to know."

"I really, really want you to know how sorry I am." Callie clenched her hands. "I'd break up with Jacob if it meant we could be friends again. I still will. Whatever it takes. I'll do it."

I looked into Callie's brown eyes and knew she meant it.

"No way," I said. "It means enough that you offered. I want you to be happy! We all deserve that."

We smiled at each other.

"Can we finally declare this awful fight over?" Callie asked.

"Yes, please. *So* over."

"I'm glad to have you back," Callie said. She put down her cup to hug me.

"Me too!" I squeezed her back. "And we're going

to take care of Jack. Together. Don't worry."

We peered through the stall guard at Jack. He'd taken a half step to the hay net and was munching.

"He can't feel too bad if he's eating," I pointed out.

"Yeah," Callie said. "That's a good sign."

I held my cup in the air. "I think we need a toast."

Callie picked up her drink.

"To getting our friendship back and to Jack," I said.

"To friendship and Jack," Callie echoed.

22

GOTTA LOVE THAT
SPARKLE

THE NEXT AFTERNOON, I FINALLY HAD TIME
to text Eric as I walked to the stable. *Guess wht? Cal & I r
friends again!*

He texted back a few seconds later. *That's great, S. :) Tell
me abt it ltr.*

I'd talked to Callie this morning and she was skipping
today's class to spend time with Jack. After the lesson, we
were going to find a practice horse for her.

I led Charm into the arena. "Ready?" I asked him.

We started toward the arena. I mounted, and he ambled
inside. Soon after, the Trio came in with their horses and
we warmed up while we waited for Mr. Conner.

When he came into the arena, Mr. Conner immediately started talking. "If your horses are warmed up," he

said, "let's canter." He turned to grab his clipboard off the table.

I slid my toe behind the girth and touched Charm's side. He moved into a smooth canter. Mr. Conner made us canter, slow to a trot, and change directions before he motioned us to slow down.

"All right, bring your horses to the center," Mr. Conner said.

We moved our horses away from the wall and stopped them in front of Mr. Conner.

"We're going to do spirals," Mr. Conner said. "You'll space your horses out in the arena. You'll begin riding in a straight line, then you'll start making a circle. Keep spiraling your horse into progressively smaller circles. When your horse can't make another turn, you may spiral out in the opposite direction."

I took up the slack in Charm's reins. Spirals would be good for us—Charm needed more work on his collection. But I *really* wanted to be on the outdoor cross-country course.

"Any questions?" Mr. Conner asked.

We shook our heads. The Trio and I separated and waited for our go.

"When you're ready," Mr. Conner said, "begin."

I squeezed my legs against Charm's sides and he walked forward. I kept him straight for a few strides before I turned him. We made a big circle, and when we hit the point where we'd started, I pressed with my inside leg and tightened the same rein. Charm responded and our circle got smaller. I thought about Callie for a second, half wishing she was here to see Charm's spirals. She'd see the exercise was helping him.

"Nice, Sasha," Mr. Conner said. "Keep it up."

I smiled. Mr. Conner walked over to Alison and Sunstruck. The Arabian danced through the spiral—Alison was working hard to keep him at a walk.

"Sit deeper and push more with your inside leg to encourage him to bend," Mr. Conner instructed Alison.

I concentrated on spiraling Charm, and after a few more rotations, his body bent into a U-shape as we made the final spiral.

"Good boy," I said, relaxing the reins. I let him straighten and rest. Julia and Heather finished their spirals, then we all started back the opposite way.

After we finished the exercise, Mr. Conner called us over to him. "Great job," he said. "So what did everyone find useful about the exercise?"

"I had to pay attention to how I used my hands and

legs," Heather said. "If I pulled too hard, the spiral got smaller faster than I wanted."

Mr. Conner nodded. "That's right. With every spiral, you had to adjust how you controlled your horse. All right. Let's take a few jumps." He pointed to Julia. "Julia, you're up first. Then Alison, Heather, and Sasha."

Julia urged Trix into a slow canter, turning her toward the first vertical. Trix took the four jumps without hesitation. Julia rode over to us, smiling.

Alison and Heather had near-perfect rides, which put pressure on me to do well.

Mr. Conner nodded at me and I let Charm trot forward. "We've got this, boy. Right?"

Charm shook his mane with confidence. I urged him into a canter and he moved toward the vertical.

Three, two, one, and up! I counted. Charm launched into the air, and the rails flashed under us. We landed and his long strides propelled us to the second vertical. Charm popped over it, flicking his tail from excitement when we hit the ground. I did a half halt to get his attention—the last thing we needed was for him to get distracted.

Charm, turning back an ear, focused and took the other jumps without a problem.

"Great!" I said, patting his shoulder as we walked back to the group.

Mr. Conner nodded at me. "Good ride, Sasha. Charm got distracted for a second, but the half halt worked to get his attention."

I relaxed into the saddle, relieved I hadn't messed up.

"See you all during the next class," Mr. Conner said.

I dismounted and led Charm out of the arena.

"Thanks, boy," I told Charm. "You were perfect."

I cooled Charm and untacked him. His chestnut coat had darkened with sweat where the wool saddle pad had been. I didn't put him away until he was clean and dry. After I fed him, I went to Jack's stall. I peered over the door at Callie as she groomed him.

"How's the patient?" I asked.

"Still sore," Callie said. "Not better yet."

I looked at Jack's hoof and nodded. "But he will be. C'mon. You've been here for a while. Let's go find a horse for you to ride."

Callie's eyes widened. She reached up to cover Jack's ears. "Don't say that in front of him!"

"Oops," I said. "Sorry, Jack."

Callie left the stall and latched the door behind her. We walked down the aisle to Mr. Conner's office. We peered through his open door and he waved us inside.

"Looking for a horse?" he asked.

Callie nodded. "Any recommendations?"

"I'd try Santana, Greenlee, and Miles," Mr. Conner said. "If you need help, come and get me."

"Santana first?" I asked, after we'd left his office. The blue roan gelding might be perfect for Callie.

"Sure."

We tacked up Santana and took him to the indoor arena. Callie rode him for fifteen minutes before shaking her head.

"Not a good fit, huh?" I called to her.

She stopped him in front of me. "No. It's not him, really. We just don't click." She dismounted and we left the arena. Mike took Santana from us and we got Miles ready. Callie rode him for almost twenty minutes, but she looked more uncomfortable on him than she had on Santana.

"We've still got Greenlee," I told her as we cooled and untacked Miles. "If she doesn't work, we'll ask Mr. Conner for different horses."

Callie was quiet as we tacked up Greenlee. I crossed my fingers when she mounted and started trotting the bay mare around the arena. Callie took Greenlee through a

few exercises, and after a few minutes, *I* wanted to try her!
The mare's temperament was as sweet as the adorable star
on her forehead. Callie grinned as she cantered Greenlee
past me.

"Looks good!" I said, glad that Callie had finally
found a horse. She needed something to keep her mind
off Jack—riding Greenlee would help.

She slowed Greenlee, nodding. "She's amazing!
Nothing like Jack, of course, but I think she'll be fun to
practice with." She hopped out of the saddle.

"Yay," I said. "You two will be great."

My phone buzzed. *Meet me in front of stbl?*

I texted back to Eric. *Sure. 1 sec.*

"I've got to go," I said to Callie. "Text me if you need
help with Jack."

"Okay. Thanks for helping me." Callie patted Greenlee's
neck.

"No prob." I walked out of the arena. I couldn't
wait to see Eric! It was about time we got to hang out.
We'd had crazy schedules for a few days and I'd missed
him.

"Hi," Eric said when he saw me.

I grinned. "Hey."

His eyes had a soft sparkle even in the faint sunlight.

I loved sparkle. Loved. It. He'd pulled a knit cap over his hair, and his black down coat was zipped all the way up. We walked toward the center of campus and I glanced at him. He was awfully quiet today.

"I helped Callie find a practice horse," I said.

Eric nodded. "Good."

We reached the courtyard and Eric paused in front of one of the stone benches. "Can we sit for a second?"

"Sure," I said, thinking this would be the perfect place for him to kiss me again. I reached into my pocket and pulled out my newest gloss—liquid Lip Smacker in Bubble Gum. I glossed my lips and sat on the bench, turning to face him.

"Sasha," Eric started. He looked down at his hands, then back at me. "Do you really want to go out with me? I honestly can't tell sometimes. I hope that you do, but if you don't, I want you to just say so."

Wh-what?!

"Eric, what are you talking about? Of *course* I want to go out with you. I like you. A lot."

My voice shook as I spoke. Why on Earth would Eric think I didn't want to go out with him?

"It's just—we still haven't gone out," Eric said. "I want to be able to take you on a real date."

"I want that too. But last time I went public with a relationship, everything got so messed up. And with Callie—we *just* got our friendship back. If I tell her about us, I'm really afraid of losing her again."

I took a breath, mad at myself for making Eric question our relationship.

"It's not . . . about Jacob?" he asked. His eyes met mine—worry had replaced the sparkle.

"Not at all," I said, shaking my head and almost laughing at how far from the truth that was. "Really. Jacob's with Callie. But even if he wasn't, I wouldn't want him back. I swear."

Eric's shoulders relaxed. He nodded and reached out to touch my hand. "I'm glad. You deserve better than that guy."

"It's not him that I'm interested in," I said. "Promise."

We looked at each other for a few seconds. I felt awful for making him worry. I'd been juggling so many things that I hadn't even noticed how upset Eric had been. Some almost-girlfriend I was.

"Okay," Eric said, grabbing my hand and pulling me up. "But I want to take you out the second you tell everyone about us. Try to stop worrying about other people breaking us up, okay? It's not going to happen."

"Deal," I said, smiling. "And . . . I'm going to tell everyone soon."

Eric smiled. "Good."

I knew now that it wasn't fair to Eric to make him wait anymore—I really did have to tell everyone. Soon.

23

PARTNERS,
AGAIN,

"I THOUGHT FRIDAY WAS *NEVER* GOING TO come," I said to Paige.

She spun in her desk chair to look at me. "I know. Longest. Week. Ever."

"At least we have something to look forward to!" I said, checking my calendar. "Only two more weeks till the *Teen Cuisine* party."

"I know!" Paige exclaimed.

We'd been planning the party whenever we had a spare second. I *might* have been using it as a diversion to keep me from worrying about when and how to spill my I'm-with-Eric news to everyone. I was in charge of decorations, which was plenty time-consuming, and I was keeping them a secret from Paige.

"Your decorations are going to be amaaaazing," I said in a teasing tone.

"Mean!" Paige stuck out her tongue. "You sure you don't want to give me a little hint?"

"No way! You'll see at the party."

Paige smiled. "Fine. But I seriously can't wait."

"You still nervous about the show?" I got up off the bed and started packing my bag for class.

"Kinda. But excited too."

I smiled. "I *know* it's going to be awesome."

I put on my coat, slinging my bag over my shoulder. "Time for film class. See you after."

"Have fun."

On my way out, I paused by Livvie's office. Her door was open and I gave her a wave. "Going to film," I told her.

"Make sure you get the film quote right," she said, looking up from her laptop.

"I'll try!"

I pushed open the door just as Jasmine and the Belles were making their way up the sidewalk toward Winchester.

"Sasha," Violet said. "You're a little early for a midnight ride."

The girls stepped around me, laughing. Ignoring them,

I kept walking. The door slammed behind me. Ugh. Was Jasmine going to be bringing them to Winchester more often? I didn't want to have to avoid more people in my own dorm.

Since it was Friday evening, the campus was busy and lights glowed from the media center. I stepped inside, rubbing my chilly fingers together. Inside the theater I sank into my seat, grateful that Jacob wasn't there yet. I sort of wanted to confront him about his riding's-not-a-sport comment, but part of me didn't even want to talk to him. Period. By the time he sat down a few minutes later, I'd settled on ignoring him.

Mr. Ramirez walked to the front of the classroom and I leaned forward. I wanted to get this quote. Jacob shifted next to me, his eyes down. Maybe he felt bad about the fight with Eric. *Well, he totally should,* I reminded myself.

"'Teenagers,'" Mr. Ramirez said. "'They think they know everything. You give them an inch and they swim all over you.'"

Ooooh! I closed my eyes. What was that from?! I'd heard it a zillion times.

"*The Little Mermaid!*" called a girl from the front row. Argh. Too slow!

"That's right! Good job," Mr. Ramirez told her. "And

that's today's film. *The Little Mermaid* debuted in 1989. We're watching it because it was the film that began the Disney Renaissance. This movie gave Disney back its critical acclaim after a string of flops. After we view it, we'll talk homework."

Mr. Ramirez turned down the lights and started the film. I squirmed through the first few minutes, uncomfortable about sitting so close to Jacob.

Even the "Under the Sea" song, one of my fave parts, didn't make me smile. The credits finally rolled and I pulled my book bag onto my lap. I wanted to be ready for a quick getaway, but Mr. Ramirez seemed to take forever to pass out homework.

"Please have those completed by next Friday," he said. "And we'll go over them in class."

I tucked the sheet into my folder, ready to bolt from the theater.

"Before you go," Mr. Ramirez said in slo-mo, "I need to assign a paper."

I let out a tiny sigh.

"You're going to write a four-page paper on one of three topics that I'll e-mail you after class," Mr. Ramirez said. "You will swap your paper with another student and you'll critique each other's work."

I looked around. I'd ask—

"To keep things simple, you'll work with your partner from the last project."

No.

Way.

Jacob and I looked at each other. He swallowed. I tried to stay calm. We were partners. Again.

"Remember, check your e-mail for all of the details about the assignment—including the deadline," Mr. Ramirez said. "Contact me with any questions. Otherwise, I'll see you next week."

I barely noticed as other students packed up to leave. The timing was *awful*. I didn't want Callie to be uncomfortable that I was paired up with her boyfriend. And Eric was already insecure about Jacob. *It's just an assignment*, I told myself. *Only one paper.* I crossed my fingers that it would be that easy.

24

DID YOU REALLY THINK
YOU HAD A CHANCE?

ON SUNDAY I MET CALLIE AT JACK'S STALL.
It had been a week since his injury, and his hoof was
almost healed. The soreness seemed to fade more with
every passing day. And each day that Jack felt a little bit
better, Callie was happier and happier. But since we'd
become friends again, there was still something I had to
do—tell her about the e-mail I'd sent to Jacob during
the clinic.

Today, I noticed that Callie's lips, usually bare at the
stable, were shiny with what I swore was Lip Smackers Lip
Frosting. I sniffed. In Coconut Cream. But then I realized
this makeup thing wasn't about Callie feeling better—it
was about Jacob! Every time she got ready to see him, she
always wore makeup.

"Look," Callie said, pointing to Jack's hoof. "He's resting his weight on it now."

I nodded. "You'll be riding him in a few days. I know it."

Callie grinned. "We'll see. I don't want to rush him."

"True. So, new gloss?" I blurted out.

"Yeah, I got it last week. I saved it for today." Callie locked Jack's stall door and stepped into the aisle.

"What's today?"

Callie paused, blinking. "Oh, um. Jacob's taking me to the movies," Callie said. "I just came to check on Jack."

"Fun," I said slowly. "I mean, good. Have fun at the movies."

"Thanks," Callie said quietly.

Tell her now about the e-mail, I told myself.

"Um, about Jacob," I said. "I wanted to tell you that, like, a long time ago—before I found out about, uh, you guys—I sent Jacob this stupid e-mail and told him that I liked him and wanted to try again. But he never got it. So if he gets it now, he should just delete it."

Callie nodded. She didn't look upset. "Okay. Thanks for telling me."

"And," I said quietly. "The Belles know about it. That's what Violet tried to blackmail me with to get me to ride Charm that night."

Callie's eyes widened. "Are you *serious*?"

I nodded.

"Forget about them," Callie said. "Look. Clean slate. As of now, nothing matters except the present and the future."

I smiled, relieved. "Okay. Same here."

When she walked away, she was practically skipping. Phew. At least she hadn't been mad about the e-mail.

But it bothered me that Callie was going to the movies. Not because she was going with Jacob—I really, truly didn't care about that now that I had Eric. It was just, why did Callie get to go on dates but I couldn't? I knew it had been *my* choice to keep my relationship with Eric on the DL, but the idea of going out on my first date ever wouldn't go away. Thinking about seeing a movie, going out to dinner, or just strolling around campus with Eric made my chest feel all fluttery. I had to tell everyone. Eric was right—I just couldn't keep worrying about this forever.

I watched Black Jack for a few more seconds before going to grab Charm's tack. Eric had invited me to ride with him, Ben, Troy, and Andy. I'd never ridden with Eric's friends before, but I knew the guys from around the stable.

"Hey, Sasha," Eric said, tossing me a smile as I entered the indoor arena.

Troy, Ben, and Andy all said hi. Like Eric, they were all intermediate riders. Ben had been Julia's boyfriend until he started dating Heather. Heather had broken up with him, but I didn't know if Ben and Julia were back together or not.

"I was thinking we should do the entire practice without stirrups," I joked.

"Ha," Andy said, laughing. "You first."

I grinned at the guys, shrugging. "Fine. Fine. We'll be wimps and ride with stirrups."

We moved our horses out along the arena wall. I eased Charm behind Luna and in front of Andy's standardbred mare. After we warmed up the horses, Ben rode into the center of the arena. I could see why Julia had liked him— he was cute *and* a good rider. And I could see him being Julia's type—pale skin, dark hair, and pretty blue eyes.

"We should play a game or something," Ben suggested.

"Like what?" Troy asked. He stopped his dappled gray gelding beside Charm.

"Musical chairs is a fun game," I said. "You guys ever play?"

Ben, Troy, and Andy nodded yeses.

Eric shook his head. "I haven't."

"It's easy," I said, looking at Eric. "Since there are five of us, we start with four traffic cones. We'll set them up in different places around the arena. Someone who isn't playing starts and stops the music. When the music stops, you race your horse over to an empty cone and dismount. If you get a cone to yourself, you're safe. You don't and you're out."

"That sounds fun," Eric said. "But no one's here to do the music."

"I'll do it," called someone from the skybox.

We all turned to see Jasmine peering down at us. She looked like a dark-haired Rapunzel with her long hair hanging down over the skybox railing.

"How long have you been there?" I snapped. Did she follow me everywhere?!

"I'll be the DJ so you guys can play your little game," she said, ignoring me.

Eric looked at me as if to say, "Your call." I didn't want to look like a bad sport in front of all the other guys, and besides, Jasmine wasn't going away, so how would anything ever get better if I always tried to exclude her? Like it or not, she was there to stay.

"Fine," I said, glancing at Jas. "If you really want to."

"Be right down," she said.

"I'll set up the cones," Andy offered. He rode over to the wall, dismounted, and picked up four cones. He started spacing them around the arena.

"This is gonna be interesting," I whispered to Eric.

"Don't worry about Jasmine," Eric said. "She won't do anything in front of all the guys."

I moved Charm away from Luna as Jasmine carried Mr. Conner's portable stereo into the arena. She put it on a table and climbed up to sit beside it. Jas folded her hands in her lap, giving us a smile that made me nervous.

Andy finished setting up the cones and we spaced our horses around the outer edge of the arena. We let the horses trot around a few times, making sure none of them were spooked by the cones. Charm didn't even look at them.

"Okay," Ben called over to Jasmine. "Whenever you're ready."

Jasmine nodded and hit play. Pop music streamed out of the speakers. Charm, loving the tunes, stretched his neck and tossed his head. I kept one eye on Jasmine and the other on the positions of the cones. In our spot at the south end of the arena, Charm and I were the farthest away from the closest cone and—

Silence.

"Go!" I yelled, urging Charm into a canter. He dashed toward the nearest cone. Andy, caught off guard, was trotting his horse toward the same cone, but he wasn't fast enough. Charm skidded to a halt and I threw myself out of the saddle. I hopped to the ground, touching my toe to the cone just as Andy jumped to the ground. Victory!

"You're out, Andy," Jasmine called.

Andy grinned sheepishly. "First one out. Bummer," he said.

"Sorry," I said, smiling at him.

I mounted Charm and rode him back to the wall. Andy, grabbing the orange cone, led his horse to the side of the arena.

Jasmine started the music, and Ben, Troy, Eric, and I trotted our horses while eyeing the cones. Again, Jasmine waited until *I* was farthest away from the cones before she pushed stop.

I heeled Charm into a canter and we cut across the center of the arena. Ben started for the same cone, but his horse started cantering a half second later than Charm. I was out of the saddle before Charm came to a full stop.

"Aw, man!" Ben said, shaking his head. But he smiled at me.

I picked up the cone and handed it to him. "Almost," I said. Ben rode over to join Andy.

We started the next round and this time, I was prepared. Jasmine hit the button the second I was in the toughest position to reach a cone. But I'd anticipated her move and Charm and I flew toward the cone the second the music stopped, taking out Troy.

"Awww," Jasmine said. "Look at that. It's Sasha and her boyfriend, Eric."

Eric and I looked at each other but didn't acknowledge her comment.

"I'm not going easy on you," Eric teased in a whisper, "just because I like you."

I dropped my jaw in mock-surprise. "You're not? Good. Then I won't feel bad when Charm and I beat you." I flipped my ponytail teasingly and rode Charm to the wall.

"Do we even have to play this round?" Jas taunted. "We all know Eric will let her win. Obvi."

"Just start the music," I said, sighing.

Jasmine waited a few seconds before she hit play. Eric and I, now at opposite ends of the arena, trotted our horses. Both of us turned our heads to stare at the last cone. I shifted in the saddle, Charm tensing beneath me. He was ready to race to the cone the second the music stopped.

We made another lap around the arena. I looked over at Eric—he had both eyes locked on the cone.

The music stopped.

"C'mon, Charm!" I said. I leaned to the right and he dug his hooves into the arena dirt and took off cantering. Eric and Luna left their side of the wall at the same time. Charm and Luna cantered for the cone—both horses knew it was a race!

A couple of strides away from the cone, I kicked my feet out of the stirrups. I squeezed my knees to stay in the saddle when Charm jerked to a halt. I halted Charm in front of the cone and threw my leg over the saddle. Eric jumped off Luna's back and we hit the ground at the same time. We lunged for the cone, but Eric's stride was longer than mine. His boot toe touched the edge of the cone a half second before mine did.

We looked up at each other and started laughing.

"Oooh!" I said, grinning. "So close!"

He winked at me. "Did you really think you had a chance?"

Forgetting that Jasmine was watching, I hit his arm. "You're lucky that your legs are longer." I sniffed. "Otherwise, I totally would have won."

We smiled at each other and turned back to Troy, Ben, Andy, and Jasmine.

"Sasha almost got you," Andy said.

Jasmine's eyes shifted from me to Eric and then back again. Then she hopped off the table, brushing off her black breeches.

"That was a total waste of time," she huffed. "You're all losers—you're not even that competitive." She stomped out of the arena.

"What was *that*?" Ben asked.

We all shrugged.

"Did she think we were going to beat each other up or something?" Andy asked.

"Guess so," Troy said, laughing.

But that hadn't been it at all. Jasmine had wanted it to be Eric and me at the end. She'd waited for him to let me win so she could call him out on being nice to me. Jas didn't know yet that Eric wasn't the type of guy to lose on purpose.

We all dismounted and led our horses out of the arena.

"Library tonight?" Eric whispered to me.

"Sure," I said.

I barely paid attention as I said good-bye to the other guys—I was already thinking about my time alone with Eric later.

25

IT'S *YOUR* REPORT CARD

ERIC AND I FOUND A TABLE ON THE FOURTH floor of the library. No matter how many times I'd been there, the inside of Canterwood's gorgeous library always took my breath away. All of the tables had dark mahogany wood and gold reading lamps adorned by forest green lampshades—Canterwood colors. The book collection was more impressive than anything I'd ever seen in my life.

I took out my math homework and started the final five questions. Eric pulled out a worn copy of *Watership Down*, taking notes while he read. We studied for half an hour and stopped only to ask each other questions every so often. The tables around us slowly filled with students.

I *had* to get everything done tonight. Monday mornings were too rushed to finish weekend homework.

"Can we sit?" someone asked me.

I looked up at Heather. She, Julia, and Alison had their arms filled with books.

"Uh," I said, pausing.

"*Hello,*" Heather said. "Holding heavy books."

"Umm, sure," I said. Eric and I pushed our extra books between us to make room for the Trio.

"We wouldn't have even asked," Alison said. "But every other table was full."

The girls sat down, and for the first time in a while, I noticed that Julia and Alison looked tired. Their usually perfect lip gloss was absent, there were circles under Julia's eyes, and Alison had a zit on her chin. I'd never seen either of them *ever* looking less than perfect.

Heather pulled out a book and started reading. I tried to concentrate on my homework, but I couldn't help watching Julia and Alison. Julia had her phone flipped open, texting. Alison, leaning over, peered at Julia's screen before pulling out her own BlackBerry.

"Omigod," Alison whispered. "Did she really just say that?"

Julia nodded. "She totally did!"

Heather glared in their direction. "Excuse me? Not wanting to flunk my class, thank you."

"Sorry," the girls whispered. They reluctantly took out their history books and bent over them.

We studied for a few minutes before Julia's phone buzzed. Heather shot her a look—daring Julia to check the message.

Julia ignored the phone for a couple of minutes, but soon she couldn't take it. Her fingers crept across the table and closed over her phone. She looked up at Heather, who just stared—her icy eyes narrowed, unmoving.

"Sorry, sorry!" Julia said. "I just can't focus!"

Alison looked up from her book and took out her own phone. "I can't either!"

Heather slammed her palms on top of her book. Everyone at the table—even Eric and me—jumped. "Don't come whining to me when you flunk your classes. I won't care!"

"We'll study later," Julia said. "Promise."

I couldn't spend another second watching Julia and Alison text.

"Ready to go?" I asked Eric.

"Definitely," he said.

We packed our books and got up from the table. I turned to Julia and Alison.

"You guys do remember that we need good grades to make the YENT, right?" I asked them.

Julia rolled her eyes. "Yes, Mom. We know."

"Fine," I said. "It's *your* report card."

Heather's mouth tightened. She flicked her eyes in a look-over-there gesture. When I did, I saw Jasmine walking toward us.

She stopped by our table and smoothed the thin blue sweater she wore over a white collared shirt. She smirked at Julia and Alison.

"Still sucking at history?" Jas asked.

"Hardly," Julia snapped. She closed her book. "We're *so* ready for the test. You?"

Jasmine tossed her wavy hair. "I think you've seen enough of my A's to know I am. You two, however . . ." She shook her head. "You'll need a miracle to pass the test."

"Like you should talk," Heather said. "You didn't pass the advanced team test."

Jasmine just glared before she walked away.

"Omigod," Julia hissed. "She is the biggest—"

"I know!" Alison whisper-yelled. "She needs to get over herself."

"I'm not even worried about the stupid test," Julia said.

She picked up her BlackBerry and started texting again.

My eyes connected with Heather's for a second. We both had to be thinking the same thing: Sure, Julia and Alison were delusional about studying, but our biggest problem? Jasmine.

26

HATE TO SAY
I TOLD YOU SO

SO GLAD WK IS 1/2 OVER. I SENT THE MESSAGE
to Eric on my way to the stable after my last class.

Me 2, he wrote back.

My phone buzzed again. This time it was from Callie.
Guess what?!?!

What?? I typed back.

I can ride Jack 2day!!!!

OMG!! C u in indr arena!! :)

At the stable, I hurried through grooming and tacking
up Charm. I was thrilled for Callie. She'd been so worried
about Jack from the second he'd injured his hoof. Now
maybe she'd stop feeling guilty.

"You get to practice with Jack again," I told Charm.
"Isn't that great?"

Charm blinked at me, rubbing his muzzle against my arm.

I put on my helmet and we walked to the indoor arena. Inside, Callie was walking Jack in lazy circles. He moved easily—not showing any signs of the injury.

"Yay!" I squealed.

"I know!" Callie grinned. "I missed him sooo much." She leaned forward to hug his neck.

"Jack's going to be stronger than ever." Jack, seeming to hear me, tossed his head and snorted. Charm sensed Jack's enthusiasm and pranced in place.

"Aww," I said, patting Charm's neck.

"They missed practicing together," Callie said.

I nodded. "Totally. Are you jumping or sticking to flatwork?"

"Flatwork only," Callie said. "I want to see how he moves for a couple more days."

"Good idea," I said. "I'll keep an eye on him too, but I'm sure he's going to be fine."

We walked Charm and Jack to the wall, then urged the horses into a trot. I watched Callie post. Her back was straight without being stiff. Her hands rested comfortably over Jack's neck. She looked flawless, as if she'd been riding Jack all along. As Charm and I passed the

window, I got a glimpse of my own reflection in the big window. I looked too ramrod straight and my heels had crept up.

No, I wasn't going to do *that* again. No way would I spend an entire lesson comparing my riding skills to Callie's. Charm and Jack made a few circles before we changed directions. But we when passed each other, I felt Callie's eyes on me. She was sizing me up too!

"Jack seems to be moving fine," I said. "How does he feel?"

"Like he never got hurt," Callie said. "I'm *so* happy!"

We both looked up when Eric walked into the arena.

"Hi," I said, with a glance at Callie.

"Hey, Eric," Callie said.

Eric walked over and stopped between our horses. He patted Charm, then rubbed Jack's neck. Charm loved Eric, and he nudged his arm when Eric patted Jack for too long.

"Charm!" I said, laughing.

"Just can't ignore you, huh, boy?" Eric teased. He stroked Charm's face with his left hand and scratched Jack's forehead with his right.

Callie and I giggled.

"Do you mind if I ride Luna in here?" Eric asked. "I

was going to take her to the outdoor arena, but it's sort of rainy."

"Fine with me," I said. Callie nodded in agreement.

"Be back in a sec," Eric said.

He returned a few minutes later with Luna. We spaced out in the arena and did our own exercises. In the far right corner, Callie walked, trotted, and halted Jack—working him on transitions. Eric, in the middle, did the spiral exercise I'd told him about. He had no problem maneuvering through the spiral at a walk, and Luna seemed to like the exercise.

I focused on my posture. Charm was in great shape, but I felt stiff. I did a few new leg and arm stretches that I'd read about the night before in *Young Rider*. After half an hour, I felt soreness start to creep into my arms and legs—time to stop.

I rode Charm into the center of the arena, and a few seconds later, Callie and Eric joined me.

"Are we good, or what?" Callie joked, as we brought the horses to a halt.

"We're definitely awesome," I said.

Eric smiled. "Want to take a few jumps?"

"Sure!" I said. Charm struck the ground with his fore-leg—he was ready!

"I'm out," Callie said. "But I'll watch you guys."

"Okay," Eric said. "Sash, want to try those three verticals?"

I nodded, pushing down my helmet. "Let's do it."

We started toward the jumps when Callie called out, "Hey!"

Eric and I looked over to see Callie riding Jack over to Jacob.

"What are you doing here?" Callie asked him. She stopped Jack a few feet away from Jacob, who stood in the middle of the arena, looking unsure where to go. He swallowed and took a step back.

"Just came to see you ride," Jacob said. "I wanted to be sure Jack was okay."

Jacob smiled at Callie but gave Eric a stony glare.

What was Jacob's *deal*?

"Jack did great," Callie told Jacob. "But I'm done. Sasha and Eric are jumping and I was just staying to watch. But we can head out and go somewhere else if you want."

Jacob shook his head. "It's fine. I'll watch too."

Callie paused for a moment. "Um, okay." She dismounted and led Jack over to the wall. Jacob followed her and didn't look at Eric or me.

This was weird! Jacob. Eric. Callie. Me. Together!

"I'll jump first," I said, trotting Charm forward. My midweek cookie break was going to be ridiculously necessary after this.

Charm was ready the second I pointed him at the course. He surged forward to the first three-foot vertical and soared over it.

"Easy," I whispered, tightening the reins. He shook his head as I eased him into a slower canter, but I held him back anyway. No way was he going to gallop. He listened to my command but swished his tail in annoyance. We got through the rest of the course cleanly. I circled him twice in progressively smaller circles to calm him down before riding him back to Eric and Callie.

"Your turn," I told Eric.

"Good job," Eric said. "You always rock at jumping."

He stroked Luna's neck before letting her go toward the course. His eyes narrowed as he looked at the jumps, and he relaxed his body. I knew he was going to go all out to prove to Jacob that riding was a sport. I crossed my fingers, hoping he would have a perfect ride.

Eric and Luna reached the first jump. Luna tucked her knees under her chest and leaped over the blue and white rails. She landed, barely making a sound, and cantered toward the next jump.

"Two more," I whispered.

Eric let Luna out a notch and rode her through the turn. He straightened her before the second vertical. Her green leg wraps flashed as she cantered to the jump. She lifted into the air, missing the top rail by inches.

"C'mon, c'mon," I muttered. Jacob, his eyes following Eric and Luna, couldn't stop watching. He'd never seen Eric ride. I'd known for a while that Eric was a star jumper, but Jacob hadn't. And Jacob didn't even need to know much about riding to be able to tell that Eric had ridden well.

Luna, relaxed and on the bit, launched into the air and propelled herself over the last jump. She landed gracefully, accepting a neck pat from Eric.

"All right!" I cheered.

Eric could totally rub this in Jacob's face. But he wasn't that kind of guy. He didn't even need to say anything to Jacob. The argument about whether or not riding was a sport had died the second Eric had finished the course.

"Seriously, great ride," I said. Charm, reaching forward, touched his muzzle to Luna's.

Callie nodded. "Yeah, nice one."

"Thanks," Eric said. He dismounted and ran up the stirrups. Jacob, now surrounded by three horses, took a step back. I could tell he wanted out of there, but he wasn't going to admit it.

"See?" I asked, looking at Jacob. "I tried to tell you that Eric was *great*."

Jacob blinked. "Yeah," he said slowly. "Good ride."

"Thanks," Eric said, gracious as usual.

"Weeelll," Callie said. "We're gonna head out. See you guys later."

Jacob nodded at us before following a safe distance behind Callie and Jack.

When Callie, Jack, and Jacob left the arena, I turned to Eric. He smiled at me and I got that floaty, tingly I-really-like-you feeling I'd been getting a lot lately.

"You were amazing," I said. "Jacob will never make another comment about riding again."

Eric stepped closer to me, and my ears thudded. "He better not. Or I really will put him on a horse."

We grinned at each other and Eric took my hand, lacing his fingers through mine. For once, I didn't care who saw us. I was just happy, in that moment, to be there with Eric.

Paige and I found an empty booth at the Sweet Shoppe. She shrugged off her raincoat and sat across from me. I'd

texted her to meet me at the Sweet Shoppe—I needed to vent to someone about Jacob showing up at the stable. Funny, the first person I'd normally speed dial would have been Callie. But we just weren't there yet.

"I think I'd go into sugar withdrawal without our Sweet Shoppe," I said.

"That Callie and Jacob thing must have been so intense," Paige said, handing me a triple fudge brownie. "You deserve, like, everything in here."

"Agreed," I said, taking a giant bite of brownie. "Jacob was so weird. I really don't know why he even came to the stable."

Paige brushed her rain-dampened hair out of her face and took a sip of her mint tea. "Probably to see if Jack was okay like he said. But still, he could have just texted or something."

I leaned back and shrugged. "That's what *I* thought. And it's superweird because I *have* to tell them about Eric and me soon. Like really soon."

Paige sipped her tea. "Um, yeah. 'Cause then you get your date."

The D word made me grin. "Exactly."

27

MY *FRIEND* ERIC

I SLID INTO MY SEAT AT FILM CLASS, PULLING out my phone to text Paige. *Ugh @ film. :S* Paige had practically shoved me out of the Sweet Shoppe so I'd get to film class on time. *Ull b fine. Watch movie & ignore him.*

I put my phone away and took out my notebook. My film paper was due in a week and a half, but I'd barely even started it. At least I'd picked a general topic that would be fun for me—famous animals in film. Jacob and I would have to meet soon to swap papers, so I really had to get started.

Jacob shuffled down the aisle and sat down. He put his book bag on the floor, turning to me. "Sash, I just wanted to say that I acted like a jerk about the riding thing. Sorry."

I stared at him. I wasn't sure what to say—I hadn't expected him to apologize. "It's fine." I went back to scribbling ideas for my paper. "Forget it."

Jacob tipped his head and looked at me like he wanted to ask me something. But I pretended to be busy, averting my eyes.

Mr. Ramirez walked to the front of the class, smiling at us. Everyone got quiet—ready to guess the film quote.

"'May the force be with you,'" Mr. Ramirez quoted.

"*Star Wars!*" I yelled along with only everyone in class.

Mr. Ramirez laughed. "I see you're all familiar with Mr. Lucas's space opera. That was pretty much a freebie. We'll be watching *Episode IV: A New Hope*, which is the first of the six films in the saga."

I sat back in my seat, listening and trying not to think about Jacob. Why did he have to be so confusing? Why did he have to be mean to Eric, and then turn around and be all apologetic and nice to me? I even saw parts of the old Jacob—the one I really liked when I first started at Canterwood. Funny, cute—even kind. Well, sometimes. But there was no excuse—and no reason—for the way he'd behaved toward Eric.

Mr. Ramirez turned down the lights and started the movie. I never thought I'd admit it, but I was actually glad

that Dad had made me watch this movie with him last year. Tonight, I wouldn't have to pay attention to the film.

When the lights came on, everyone gathered their stuff. I hadn't looked at Jacob once since the beginning of class.

"Sash—" Jacob started.

I got up, grabbed my bag, and hurried down the aisle, hoping I could pretend I hadn't heard him. He didn't need to apologize again about the riding thing.

I pulled out my phone to text Paige, hoping Jacob would get the signal that I was busy. Besides, it was also totally necessary to check on Paige. The *Teen Cuisine* party was in a week and she was slipping into freak-out mode. I was afraid of going back to Winchester and finding our room stuffed with cupcakes. Paige's way of dealing with nerves? Baking zillions of batches of cupcakes.

If u r near oven, step away &— I started to text.

"Sasha, c'mon," Jacob said, catching up with me. He walked along beside me.

I closed my phone. "What?" I asked.

We slowed and looked at each other.

"I've been trying to ask you something. Are you—" Jacob started, and then stopped abruptly. When I looked up, I saw why he'd stopped talking.

Callie and Eric.

They stood a few feet apart. Callie, arms crossed over her cropped black blazer, looked through the door to the theater as if she was waiting for someone. Eric's hands were shoved deep in his pockets, and he smiled when he saw me.

I waved at them, unsure what else to do.

"Hey," I said to Callie and Eric.

"Hi," Callie said. Jacob walked over to stand by her.

Eric smiled at me again. I gave him a quick smile but stayed where I was—feet away from him.

"Good class?" Callie asked

"Yeah," Jacob said. "It was fine."

I nodded. "Totally fine."

"We're going to the Sweet Shoppe," Callie said. "What are you doing?"

I looked at Callie and Jacob. What did I say?! "My *friend* Eric and I are going to . . ."

Eric just looked at me, not helping at all.

Callie and Jacob stared, waiting for me to finish my sentence.

"I was walking by and remembered Sasha had a class here," Eric said, finally jumping in. "I'm going right by Winchester if you want to walk with me."

I just nodded.

"See you later," Callie said to me.

I smiled and held myself back from running out of the lobby. Eric was behind me as I shoved open the door and stomped onto the sidewalk.

"Why did you come to *film*?" I cried. "You know Jacob's in my class."

Eric stopped, looking at me. "Sasha, I just came to see *you*. It's Friday. I thought we could do something later. I honestly didn't even think about Callie or Jacob."

I sighed. He'd come to the media center to be nice and I'd acted like a jerk.

"I'm sorry," I said. "I'm being ridiculous. I'm glad to see you too."

Eric didn't say anything, and we started walking again. We were heading down the winding sidewalk, making our way to Winchester. I could feel the empty space between us and I knew I was supposed to be the one to fill it up. But I wasn't sure what to say.

"Really," I whispered. "I'm sorry."

Eric looked at me. "It's okay. I know you just want to tell Callie on your own time."

"I do. I just don't know why I can't make myself tell her. But I really want to."

Eric shrugged. "She's your friend. And she's with Jacob. I really don't think she'll be mad at you. You never lied to her—you just didn't tell her the truth right away. And I promise, no one is going to break us up. Unless . . ."

"Unless?" I prompted.

Eric let out a breath. "Unless Jacob is the one you don't want finding out about us."

"*What*?" But when I thought about it, it made perfect sense why Eric would think that. "Oh, Eric, *no*. I like *you*."

Eric looked at me. He needed me to do something. Now.

"I'm going to announce it at Paige's party," I declared. "That way everyone will know at once."

Eric smiled and narrowed his eyes at me, like maybe I was playing a trick on him. "Are you sure about that?"

I looked into his eyes, willing him to believe me. "In exactly one week," I said, "everyone is going to know that—"

"You're my girlfriend." Eric smiled.

28

GUEST LIST

THE WINCHESTER COMMON ROOM HAD BECOME the unofficial party-planning headquarters for the *Teen Cuisine* premiere party. Paige and I had been talking last-minute details for the past couple of hours. The planning was a welcome relief from an insane week of papers, quizzes, and too many books to read. At least I'd finally written my film paper—now I just had to set up a time to meet Jacob for my critique.

"Flavored sparkling water. Yes or no?" Paige asked.

"Yes," I said. "Definitely."

I twirled my pen in the air. Tomorrow was it. The day I'd tell everyone about Eric and me. I wavered between nerves and excitement. But after tomorrow, Eric and I could finally go on our first official date. A real date. Oh, my God. I grinned hugely.

"Sasha?" Paige asked.

"What?"

"I was saying," Paige said, "that I have to finish baking the last batch of cupcakes tomorrow morning."

"I'll help you if you want," I offered.

Paige shook her head. "Uh, thanks, but we know how that would turn out."

"What?" I faked shock. "How?"

"Oh, I don't know. But I'm guessing it would involve a fire."

We both laughed until our eyes teared.

"Fine," I said, sticking out my tongue. "I'll stay far away from your precious food."

I double-checked my decoration list. Tomorrow, I had to sneak off to the media center to put everything up. I couldn't wait to see Paige's face when she walked into the room.

"Are you going to be okay with Callie, Jacob, *and* Eric there?" Paige asked.

I considered telling Paige about my announcement plan, but decided against it. She was nervous enough about her party—I didn't want her to worry about me and Callie.

"I'll be fine. It's your party. No one's going to mess it up."

"'Kay. But you have to tell me if things get weird. Promise?"

"Promise. And I think—" I stopped talking when Jasmine walked into the room. I thought about how she really *had* worn all of those clothes that she'd brought in her thousands of suitcases. I hadn't seen her in the same shirt twice. Tonight, she wore a soft lilac wrap sweater and a pair of black low-rise pants. Her Sidekick was pressed against her ear.

"But I want them to—" Jasmine stopped talking when she saw us. "Hold on."

With an exaggerated huff, Jas turned and walked back out of the room.

Paige and I looked at each other.

"What's up with her?" Paige asked.

I sighed. "No clue. She's probably plotting something against the Trio."

"Well, if anyone can handle Jas," Paige said, "it is Heather."

"I hope so," I said, remembering the Belles' intervention in the cafeteria.

Jasmine was obviously up to something. I'd just

have to cross my fingers that Heather would handle whatever it was. The Trio and I weren't friends, but it was still us—the real Canterwood riders—against Jasmine.

29

RED-CARPET
READY

PARTY NIGHT HAD FINALLY ARRIVED AND *I* was more nervous than Paige! I'd been trying on clothes for an hour, desperate for the right I'm-dating-Eric outfit. Paige, of course, had chosen her dress last week and was putting it on in the bathroom. She'd kept it a surprise till now.

I shifted a giant pile of clothes from my bed to the floor for maximum room. Thankfully, my mom wasn't here to see the disaster zone. Everything was just too girly, too stuffy, too ruffly, or too blah. I needed something *perfect*.

"Okay," Paige called through the bathroom door.

"Finally! Get out here."

The door opened and Paige stepped out, clasping her hands. "What do you think?"

She looked premiere party perfect. She'd chosen a black and ivory raw silk bubble-hem dress that came up just above her knees. The strapless style showed off her porcelain-pale shoulders. On her feet, she wore a new pair of black ballet flats—satin with elegant half bows.

"Oh, Paige," I breathed. "Wow."

"Really?" Paige smoothed her dress.

I nodded. "It's gorgeous."

Paige smiled. "Yay! But what is this?" She looked at my ever-growing *no* pile. "We've got to find you something!"

"Everything in my closet is horrible and gross," I moaned. "I'm about to put on my pajamas."

"Okay, but let's try something else before we pull out the velour tracksuit."

"Like what?" I asked, tossing more clothes on the floor.

Paige walked over, grabbed my hand, and dragged me away from my closet. "You need to visit the hottest store in town."

"I don't have time to go shopping!" I said. "We have to leave in an hour!"

Paige pulled open her closet doors. "Lucky for you, Paige's Closet is always open. It's nearby and the owner is, like, the most amazing person ever. Get over here!"

I walked over to Paige, laughing.

Paige peered into her closet, looking over a dozen dresses. She pulled out a few, shook her head, and put them back. I was seriously beginning to contemplate the pajama idea when Paige smiled.

"Got it!" Paige said. She pulled out a simple little black dress with a halter neckline.

I looked it over. It was a pretty dress . . . but sort of plain. "Are you sure?" I asked.

Paige rolled her eyes and handed it to me. "Just put it on—I'm telling you. I'll warm up the flatiron while you change."

I slipped the dress over my head and fastened the closure at the neck. I looked at myself in the mirror. What I saw practically made my mouth drop. It had looked ordinary on the hanger, but once I'd put it on, it was stunning. The halter neck showed off my toned-from-riding arms. The A-line cut was flattering for my figure—skimming over my hips in just a slight curve. It was the most beautiful I'd ever felt in a dress.

Paige grinned behind me. "I knew that dress would be perfect."

"I love it," I agreed. "Okay, now that you've dressed me, you sit and I'll do your hair."

Paige took her long hair out of its ponytail and sat at her desk chair. I clipped back sections of her hair and started to flatiron.

My mind wandered to Eric. I couldn't wait for him to see me in this dress.

Once I was finished, Paige and I swapped seats and she smoothed my hair with the flatiron but was careful not to make it too straight. My golden brown hair was naturally wavy and Paige was sure to keep the loose waves intact.

"Makeup time," I said, once my hair was finished.

Paige checked her watch. "We've got to leave in half an hour. I feel like I should already be there setting up!"

"No way. It's *your* party. Everything will be ready when you get there, trust me."

A few hours ago, I'd sneaked off to the media center when Paige had been on a phone call with her *Teen Cuisine* producer. I'd met Annabella and Suichin—two of our friends from Winchester. We'd taken the party decorations from storage and had spent most of the afternoon decorating.

Paige took a breath. "Okay."

We did our makeup, taking longer than usual to apply dabs of concealer, smoky gray eyeliner, iridescent eye shadow, and peachy blush. I tried four lip glosses before settling on a rosy pink with a hint of shimmer.

I looked like someone's girlfriend.

I put on silver ballet flats and grabbed my phone.

Can't wait 2 tell every1 abt us. I texted Eric.

:) C u soon.

I put my phone in my purse, then turned to Paige.

"Ready?" I asked.

Paige swallowed. "Yes. No. Are we?"

"Yes," I said, smiling.

We pulled on our coats and waved at Livvie as we walked out of Winchester. Linking arms, we hurried across the chilly campus. The streetlamps cast a warm, soothing glow over campus. I tipped my face to the sky and looked at the stars—they were bright in the night sky. I just *knew* tonight was going to be perfect. I almost skipped up the sidewalk.

"And spring is supposed to be here when?" Paige asked teasingly.

"It's April. This *is* spring," I said.

"Well, it's cooold!"

We hurried to the media center.

"Look!" I said, pointing ahead of us.

On the glossy hardwood floor of the hallway, a red

carpet ran along the center. The carpet went right into the biggest, best TV room in the entire media center.

"It's really a red carpet!" Paige squealed. "I heart it!"

"Be cool," I whispered, looking ahead. "Paparazzi!"

They were all friends of Paige's who had offered to play photogs. They held up digital and cell phone cameras.

"Paige! Paige Parker!" they shouted. "Look here! Paige!"

"Omigod," Paige said, her face blushing. "Guys!"

Paige, playing it up, stopped and struck a pose. We made faces at the camera, giggling, and let the boys take a bunch of pics before we started walking again.

I turned around and gave them a thumbs-up. They'd been perfect paparazzi!

"That was just too awesome," Paige said.

"You'll want them to follow you everywhere now."

Paige and I walked up to the door of the party room. A guy in front of the door held up his hand. He totally looked the part of a security guard with dark sunglasses, a pressed black suit, and a Bluetooth earpiece. Behind him, a red velvet rope held by two brass poles blocked the doorway.

"IDs, please," he said.

Paige giggled. "Ryan, seriously. Do you need IDs from the party star and her BFF?"

Ryan didn't say anything. He just stared. Okaaay, he was playing this part *really* well! A few seconds later, he finally lowered his sunglasses and winked at us. "My mistake, Miss Parker. Please, go right inside."

When Ryan stepped aside, he revealed a sign on the door. The silver sparkly letters read PAIGE PARKER'S TEEN CUISINE PREMIERE PARTY.

"Oooh! Beautiful!" Paige said.

Paige and I grinned at each other as Ryan unhooked the rope. He pulled open the door, waving us inside. I let Paige walk in first.

"Oh, my God!" she cried. She froze in her tracks and I almost bumped into her.

"Not bad, huh?" I asked.

Paige had to take a breath. "It's fantastic!"

And she was right, if I do say so myself . . .

The TV room had been transformed into a sleek party space. Everything had been decorated with silver and plum—the *Teen Cuisine* logo colors. Silver runners accented the dark wooden tables, gauzy fabric had been draped over the lamps to create ambiance, and candles flickered softly on the tables. One of Paige's friends had called the *Teen Cuisine* studio and asked for promotional posters. The studio had been happy to oblige—they sent

five different shots of Paige with the *Teen Cuisine* logo and we'd put them up on the walls.

A giant plasma screen TV was set on the Food Network for Kids channel. The room was packed—it seemed like everyone in our entire grade was here!

"Hi, Paige!" Geena said, coming over to us. She hugged Paige. I'd met Geena a couple of times when Paige had invited her over to the common room to test recipes or do homework.

"Hey, is Erin here?" Paige asked.

"Yeah, she's by the snacks," Geena said. "C'mon." She pulled Paige over to the food table.

I grabbed a glass of sparkling apple cider and looked around the room. Annabella and Suichin chatted with Paige and Geena. Nicole, an intermediate rider, was talking to one of Paige's friends from Orchard—Callie and the Trio's dorm. I didn't see Heather, Julia, or Alison yet. Paige had refused to snub them, so they'd been invited. She didn't want to be rude. Eric wasn't here yet either.

I sipped my cider, looking around the room for anyone else that I knew. In the center of the room, by the food table, I saw *them*. Callie and Jacob. Callie, looking stunning in a belted cranberry minidress, had her arm around Jacob's waist. Jacob gazed adoringly at her and Callie

leaned over to snuggle up to his shoulder. It would be a lie to say I wasn't jealous that Callie and Jacob got to be together like that in front of everyone. But after tonight, Eric and I could do that too.

Jacob waved at a guy by the TV, whispered something to Callie, and then walked over to his friend. Callie turned slightly and saw me. She weaved around the other people and stood beside me.

"Great party," she said.

"Paige totally deserves it," I said. "She's still nervous about everyone seeing the show."

Callie shook her head. "Please! Paige is a pro. She's going to be amazing."

"Agreed. And I love your hair," I said. Callie's raven hair hung in loose, soft layers around her shoulders.

Callie smiled at me, but her attention was noticeably on Jacob. "Thanks."

I took a gulp of cider. *Just tell her*, I told myself. But did I blurt it out? Or lead into it somehow? And how would I even start something like this?

"Oooh! Nicole's here," Callie said. "I'm going to talk to her for a sec."

"Okay," I squeaked.

Phew. That at least bought me a few more minutes.

I took another sip of cider and looked around for Eric. He still wasn't here yet. But the Trio had arrived. Julia, Heather, and Alison stood by the food table. Alison put two pink cupcakes on her plate before following Heather and Julia to the couches in front of the TV.

I texted Eric. *WRU?*

My phone buzzed. *IL B L8. SRY. 10 mins.*

K. C u.

Disappointed, I closed my phone and looked up right into Jacob's eyes. I jumped back, sloshing my drink and spilling a tiny bit on the floor.

"Oh, hey," I said. "You scared me!"

Jacob smiled. "Sorry. So, um, who were you texting?"

"Just . . . my dad."

I was the worst liar! Who texted her father at a party? Apparently, I did.

"You look . . . ," Jacob started to say, but stopped.

Looked what? Pretty? Horrible? Guilty?

"I meant, uh, your dress is nice," Jacob finished.

"Thanks," I said. Was he still supposed to say that stuff to me? But then I remembered the way he'd been staring at Callie earlier and I knew the answer—Jacob was just being polite.

He looked nice all dressed up in black pants and a long-sleeve polo shirt.

"Well," he said. "See you later." He brushed his hair out of his eye like he always did when he was nervous.

"Later," I said in my fake-cheery tone.

Jacob shot me a look as if he knew something was up, but walked over to join Callie without saying anything.

At least Paige was having fun. She stood by the coffee table in front of the TV, gesturing and laughing.

I finished my drink and grabbed a new one even though the bubbles from the cider weren't doing much to calm my stomach. I checked the time on my phone. Eric should have been here by now.

Someone with cold fingers grabbed my arm and pulled me toward the back of the room.

"Hey!" I protested when I turned to see Heather. "What are you doing?"

She let me go and took my glass. "What are *you* doing? You've had, like, eight glasses of cider in five minutes." She peered at me. "And you're kind of pale and sweaty. Did Jas do something?"

I shook my head. "No, Jasmine wasn't even invited. But isn't the party great?"

"Stop trying to change the subject," Heather said.

"Something's wrong. Not that I even know why I'm asking."

She smoothed her silver metallic satin dress. I was *not* going to talk about Callie and Jacob with her. It's not like we were friends. And besides, she'd blackmail me with it somehow.

Heather sighed. "Fine. I don't have time to play this game. It's Callie, Jacob, and Eric."

Okaaay.

"What? No, it's not," I lied. "I'm totally fine."

Heather rolled her eyes, but her frown softened. "Yeah. You look so awful that I can totally tell you're fine."

"Thanks," I snapped. "Glad to know I look 'awful.'"

"That's not what I meant. But c'mon. I know you're with Eric."

Her last sentence made me freeze. I couldn't believe it. Heather had already messed up one of my relationships, and now she was about to do it again!

"No," I said. "I'm not. We're just—"

"If you say 'friends,' your drink is going to wind up on your head." Heather tilted my glass in her hand.

I stared at her, trying to figure out how to fix this. But after the moronic lie I'd told Jacob about texting, I knew I wasn't a good enough liar to fool Heather.

"Fine," I whispered. "I'm with Eric. So what?"

"So nothing. Lucky for you, I don't hate you at this very moment. I'm not going to tell anyone."

I blew out a breath.

"But seriously, if I noticed something going on, Callie will too, if she hasn't already. She really doesn't know?"

I shook my head.

"Just tell her, Silver." Heather straightened and squinted at me. "And stop drinking so much cider. The sugar is making you act even weirder than usual."

She walked away, her kitten heels clicking on the floor.

I stood in the back of the room, trying not to panic. Heather knew, but she wouldn't tell anyone. Not unless I made her mad between now and my announcement.

"There you are."

When I turned, Eric stood there, smiling at me. And oh, my God. He looked gorgeous. He was wearing black pants, an open black blazer, and a dark gray T-shirt. But it wasn't just the clothes. Eric always looked so cool and calm, so confident.

"I'm so glad you're here," I said.

"Me too. Sorry I was late." He shook his head. "My dorm advisor held a last-minute meeting about keeping our rooms clean and he talked forever."

I grinned. "And did you guys *need* that talk?"

"Maybe," Eric said, laughing.

I shook my head, but Eric just kept smiling at me.

"You look amazing," he said, his voice soft. "Really great."

I'd been waiting all night to hear him say that. "So do you," I said.

"Tonight's going to be fun." Eric looked around. "Have you talked to Callie yet?"

I paused. The nerves came back. "Um, well, not yet. The show's about to start. After?"

I knew I couldn't keep stalling all night, but I needed more time.

"Sounds good. Let's go get a seat."

Eric followed me to the front of the room. We skirted around the coffee table, now full of half-empty cups and plates, and sat on the couch. I squeezed next to Eric, trying to remember to breathe when his knee brushed against mine.

"Best seat in the house," Eric whispered to me.

My face went pink. He *was* talking about me and not his proximity to the TV, right?

Paige sat on the opposite couch with Annabella and Suichin next to her. She grinned at me and crossed her fingers.

"It's going to be awesome," I said to Paige. "Stop worrying!"

Paige pointed to the wall clock. "At least I only have to freak out for a few more seconds!"

Everyone who had been getting a drink or snack hurried over to get in front of the TV. People sat on the floor, pulled up chairs, and piled on the couches.

And that's when Jacob slid into the seat next to me. Callie sat next to him, but still—Jacob couldn't have picked any other seat?! Eric turned away from the TV and glanced at Jacob. Jacob ignored Eric's gaze and kept his eyes focused on the TV. Suddenly, the *Teen Cuisine* intro music started to play.

Everyone stopped talking and we all turned to the screen as Paige appeared.

"Hi, I'm Paige Parker," said TV Paige. "Welcome to *Teen Cuisine!*"

"Oh, my God," someone whispered. "You're really on TV!"

Paige blushed and half covered her eyes with her hands.

"I'm the new host of *Teen Cuisine*," TV Paige continued. "I'm so excited to be able to cook with you every week. We'll have so much fun making new recipes and trying different foods. Stay tuned for my first breakfast food—wild-blueberry muffins with lemon icing!"

The channel cut to a commercial and the room erupted in applause.

"Yaaaay, Paige!" I cheered. "You're a total TV star."

Annabella elbowed Paige. "Hello! We so knew her when."

Paige smiled and waved us off. "Oh, whatever," she said. But I could tell she loved it.

We teased her through the commercial, but everyone fell silent when the show came back on. I settled in my seat, glad to lose myself in Paige's show.

30

THREE STRIKES

TEEN CUISINE WAS HALF OVER AND I'D BECOME too absorbed with the show to even care where I was sitting. I'd kept my eyes on the TV or Paige, so I hadn't looked to see if the guys were trading weird glances behind my back.

"And now," TV Paige said, "we'll make icing." She smiled at the camera. "You'll need two sticks of butter, a jar of Marshmallow Fluff, a cup of confectioners' sugar, and a teaspoon of vanilla extract."

TV Paige reached for a pink mixing bowl. "Next, we—"

"Cozy?" someone whispered in my ear.

I turned and saw Jasmine.

"Be right back," I whispered to Eric. He nodded, but his focus was on the TV.

I slipped away from the crowd.

Jasmine, standing near the back window, smiled as I walked over. She looked sweet—how misleading—in a pearly pink sweater and ruffled black skirt.

"Why are you even here?" I asked. "This is a private party."

Jas folded her arms. "Really? Well, Paige invited me."

"No, she didn't. Paige would never invite you."

"Oh, but she did. I reminded her that I'm the new girl with no friends and she asked me to come. Almost begged me, really."

I sighed. Of course. Jas knew Paige was too polite to say no.

"Whatever. I'm going back to watch the show." I turned away from Jas and started to walk away.

"Back to your boyfriend?"

I whipped back around to face Jasmine. "So what if he is?" I asked.

"Then I hope you're very happy with him," Jas said, smirking. "The second Callie finds out, he'll be all you have. Oh, and Paige too. Unless she becomes *my* BFF."

"Paige will never be your best friend," I said. "And Callie will understand about Eric—not that it's any of your business."

Jas shook her head. "Oh, Sasha. You really shouldn't be so mean to me."

"Or what?" I challenged. "You'll tell everyone?"

Jas smiled sweetly. "Of course not, Sash. You are!"

"I was going to anyway," I snapped. "You're not forcing me to do anything. And sorry to disappoint, but Callie will understand when I tell her."

Jasmine laughed and the *Teen Cuisine* music swelled in the background. "You're so clueless, Sasha Silver from Union. But I'll give you a little tip."

Jasmine looked around and leaned closer to me. I could smell her strawberry-scented gloss. "Yesterday, I overheard Callie and Jacob talking in the hallway. Jacob told Callie something was going on with you. Callie agreed, but she said you'd just become friends again and you'd tell her if something was wrong."

"Okay, so what?"

"So guess what Jacob said to that?"

I held out my hand in the universal if-you're-going-to-say-something-just-say-it gesture.

Jas smirked, relishing this moment for sure.

"He told Callie that he thought you were dating Eric," she said.

I swallowed. So Jacob had known! That's why he'd been acting so weird.

"So?" I shrugged, attempting nonchalance.

"Callie *freaked*. She said that if it was true, she couldn't believe you'd hide that from her after what happened between you. Then she said you'd probably been with Eric all along and had lied to her. She was furious. Jacob was too. He told her you'd probably been lying the whole time."

My stomach flip-flopped and I felt dizzy. This was the worst thing possible thing to have happened tonight! I couldn't tell Callie anything now—not if she was already angry. It would ruin the whole night.

"But why didn't Callie say anything to me?" I asked.

"She wanted to, but Jacob suggested they wait. The sooner *you* told *them*, the better 'friend' you really were."

"I don't believe you. I'd know if Callie was that upset about something," I ventured.

"Yeah. Just like you knew about Callie and Jacob."

I froze. Jas was right. And Heather had been right about the cider—it was swirling in my stomach and making me sick.

"So, you've got two choices," Jas said with a grin. "You've got a week to face Callie and tell her about Eric, or I will. I almost want to make you tell her *now*, but seeing you sweat for a whole week sounds like a lot more fun."

230

She brushed her shoulder against mine as she walked away and slipped out of the room.

I stood in the back for a few minutes, trying to calm down. Either way I looked at it, I was going to lose Callie. The second I told her about Eric, she'd accuse me of lying and our friendship would be gone forever. But if I let Jas confirm Callie's suspicions . . . I shuddered. I couldn't let that happen.

I brushed my hair back and tiptoed back to the couch. Everyone was busy watching the show and no one had heard my chat with Jasmine.

"Everything okay?" Eric whispered.

"Fine," I said.

He nodded and turned back to the show.

I watched the rest of *Teen Cuisine* in a trance, clapping like a robot when it ended.

"You were so great," I told Paige, hugging her. "I'll be back. I forgot my lip gloss, so I'm running back to Winchester for a sec."

"Okay," Paige said, her face flushed from everyone's applause. "Hurry back!"

I nodded and started to the door. Phew. Paige had bought my lie and, hopefully, she'd be too busy to notice when I didn't come back. Eric was by the snack table talking to Troy. If I could just slip out without him seeing me, I'd text him when I got back to Winchester. I'd tell him I'd gotten sick and had to leave. My fingers closed on the door handle and I started to pull it open.

"Sasha."

I ducked my head at the sound of Eric's voice. So. Close.

"You're not trying to ditch me, are you?" he teased.

"No way," I said, touching my stomach. "I just feel sort of sick. I'll text you when I get back to Winchester. I want you to stay and enjoy the party."

Eric looked at his shoes, then back at me. His eyes were dark and his stare critical—I'd never seen that expression on his face. "I wish you'd just tell me the truth."

"The truth?" I asked.

Someone turned up the TV volume and Eric leaned closer to me. "The truth about why you're keeping us a secret from everyone. I . . ." Eric paused, looking down and then back at me. "I can't tell anymore if you really like me or if you're waiting for . . ."

"That's not it," I whispered, panic pounding in my chest. "I wanted to tell everyone, I swear! But when Jasmine showed up tonight, she told me that she'd overheard Callie say she thought we were together and that I'd been lying all along. I freaked out. I'm sorry. I—"

Eric shook his head and I closed my mouth, ending my ramble. I didn't want to keep arguing here—a couple of Paige's friends were already glancing in our direction.

"Look, Sasha. I really don't know what to believe anymore. How am I supposed to feel that you want me to be your secret boyfriend? According to you, *everyone* knew it when you liked Jacob."

"Yes, and that's why things went so wrong," I said, trying not to throw up.

Eric took a step back. "If you trusted me, then you'd know this is going to be different. *I'm* different."

"Of course I trust you! It's not about that at all. I was so happy with the way things were and didn't want anyone to mess it up."

I tried not to cry. I'd made Eric feel awful and I hadn't even seen it.

I opened my mouth, but Eric interrupted. "Sasha, I really like you. But right now, I just need some time to think."

"But—" I started. This couldn't be happening. Eric had to believe me that it was never about Jacob. Fear crushed my chest. I couldn't lose Eric.

"You stay." Eric stared at me, his face blank. "I'm going to head out."

I swallowed. "Okay." Tears blurred my vision. "But please believe me, Eric—it was never about Jacob," I choked out. I watched as he pulled open the door.

I turned back to the party—everyone's faces a blur.

I'd just hurt one of the people that I cared about most. I'd had three perfect opportunities to tell the truth—the picnic with Callie, the night at film when we'd all been together, and tonight—and I'd refused all of them. In horse show world, three refusals meant elimination. Eric would probably never speak to me again.

31

I HATE MONDAYS

WHEN I PULLED ON MY RIDING BOOTS FOR Monday morning's lesson, I thought about how torturous the weekend had been. For two days, I agonized about Eric and Callie. I'd picked up the phone to call Callie a million times, but hung up every time. Eric's plea to give him room had flashed in my brain whenever I'd started to text him. I hadn't sent one message.

"You sure I did the right thing this weekend?" I asked Paige, slipping into my coat.

"Absolutely," Paige said. "You were going to let Jasmine bully you into telling Callie. You need it to come from you *wanting* to tell Callie, or it'll make things worse. And with Eric, you were just giving him the space he wanted."

"But every second I wait, Eric could be getting more upset," I said. "I feel awful."

Paige shook her head. "Eric's not mad at you, Sash. He was just hurt. When he calms down, he'll realize that he would never want you to ruin your friendship with Callie just to publicize your relationship."

"But I still have to tell her. And everyone else."

"You do," Paige said. "But not because Jas forced you. I mean, what if she's lying?"

I paused. "I do believe her. I don't know why, but I just do."

I ducked into the bathroom to brush my hair. At least Paige's party hadn't been ruined. Just like I'd hoped, she hadn't noticed that I'd ducked out until five minutes before the party was supposed to end. She'd had a perfect night and I was glad I hadn't messed it up with my boy drama.

But now I had to go riding. Callie would be there and I still didn't know what to say.

"It's going to be fine," Paige said before I left for the stable. "Really."

"You're the best, thank you," I said.

I walked slow enough to the stable that I was almost late when I got there. Charm, sensing my worried mood, was extra sweet to me as I tacked him up. His big brown eyes followed me as I unhooked the crossties. He nosed me and rubbed his cheek resting on my shoulder.

"Thanks, boy," I said. "I needed that." I hugged Charm's neck, inhaling his sweet hay-and-grain scent. I let him go and we walked to the arena. I mounted, peering through the window.

Everyone was already warming up inside.

"What should we do?" I whispered to Charm. "Do we go in or skip?"

Charm looked in the direction of the arena. Sigh. I waited a few more seconds before I let him walk through the entrance. Callie's back was to me as she trotted Jack along the wall.

I let Charm walk through the center of the arena, urging him toward Jack. I wanted to tell Callie that we needed to talk. But strides away from Callie, Mr. Conner walked into the arena. He motioned for us to line up in front of him. Callie and I ended up at opposite ends of the line.

"Let's get right to work, girls," he said. "I want to run through flatwork, then try something new."

"New?" Julia asked. She rubbed Trix's neck when the mare sidestepped.

"We're going to try arena cross-country," Mr. Conner

said. "It's too dangerous for us to get on the real outdoor course, but I want you to practice. While you warm up in here, Mike, Doug, and I are going to set up a course in the outdoor arena."

Even my worry about Callie couldn't stop me from smiling. Charm and I were *finally* about to do cross-country.

"I'll be back in a few minutes," Mr. Conner said.

I angled Charm behind Sunstruck and he started trotting. There was no way I'd be able to talk to Callie during a lesson. I also didn't want to risk getting kicked out for talking.

When Mr. Conner came back, he took us through a few exercises. We were all eager to get through flatwork and try arena cross-country.

"All right," Mr. Conner said finally. "Let's stop and talk jumping."

I pulled Charm next to Aristocrat.

"In a minute, we're going to head to the outdoor arena. There's a short course that will give you the feel of cross-country. While you wait, stay out of the arena so your horse doesn't have time to become familiar with the obstacles."

Heather and I exchanged glances. We both excelled at cross-country.

"Wipe that I'm-number-one-and-I-know-it look off your face," Heather whispered. "You're not the only one who's good at cross-country."

"We'll see," I whispered back.

"Let's go," Mr. Conner said. We followed him out of the stable and to the outdoor arena. Weak sunshine spilled over the grounds and the spring sky was cloudless. Brighter, greener grass was taking over the dry winter grass. The rolling hills would soon be clover green.

I was glad to get out of the confining indoor arena—it felt especially small when you thought someone was mad at you.

"Alison," Mr. Conner said. "You may go first. Everyone else, please wait by the entrance."

Callie, Heather, Julia, and I gathered our horses by the fence. I looked out at the arena. Mr. Conner hadn't been kidding—it was like a mini-cross-country course! He'd set up log piles, hay bales, a faux ditch, shrubs, barrels, and a table.

Alison trotted Sunstruck through the entrance, squeezing with her knees. She had to keep pressure on Sunstruck, who sometimes spooked at new obstacles, to get him through the course. But when she kept Sunstruck calm, the palomino seemed to float over the jumps.

Alison eased Sunstruck into a canter and he jumped over the log pile without hesitation. Strides before the hay bales, he started to weave.

"He's gonna run out," Julia whispered. "There's no way she'll get him over that."

Alison urged him forward with her hands and seat, sitting deep in the saddle. Sunstruck's ears flicked back and forth and he shifted sideways with every step.

"More leg!" Mr. Conner called.

Alison, nodding once, urged Sunstruck forward. They reached the hay bales and at first I thought he would refuse. He rocked back on his haunches, almost freezing for a second before popping into the air. The form wasn't pretty, but he made it over the scary bales.

Sunstruck's confidence was up after he cleared the bales. Alison got him over the rest of the jumps without a problem.

"Excellent," Mr. Conner told her. "That was tough. It took great concentration on your part to get Sunstruck through the course. You should be proud of that ride."

Alison blushed and rubbed Sunstruck's neck.

"Heather, when you're ready," Mr. Conner said.

Heather and Aristocrat put on a strong performance just as I knew they would. Aristocrat, always a powerful jumper, was in top form and he sailed over every obstacle with room to spare. Heather rode him back to us, smiling.

Mr. Conner nodded at Julia. She got Trix over the logs and hay bales. Trix started to slow as they approached the "ditch," which was a brown tarp held down by two jump poles. The horse couldn't tell the difference between the dirt-colored tarp and a hole.

"Keep her moving," Mr. Conner said. "Don't let her slow down."

But Julia reacted too late. Trix, already spooked by the ditch, broke into a trot. Julia couldn't get her back to a canter. Trix slid to a halt before the jump, and Julia grabbed fistfuls of mane to keep herself from falling forward over Trix's head. She let Trix back up, then turned her to Mr. Conner.

"Sorry," she muttered. "I didn't get her going fast enough."

"It's okay," Mr. Conner said. "Start again at the hay bales. Move her forward with your legs and seat. She's going to try to get away with stopping again, so be ready."

Julia nodded and tapped Trix with her heels. Trix took the hay bales, and Julia urged her into a faster canter. I watched as Trix's stride shortened and her back tensed. Julia pushed Trix forward with her seat, encouraging the mare to keep moving. Just when I thought Trix would slam to a halt, she leaped into the air and cleared the ditch.

"Yes!" Alison whispered.

Julia and Trix completed the rest of the course and rejoined us. Alison high-fived Julia.

"Good job," Mr. Conner said. "You didn't let the first mistake rattle you. You kept enough pressure on her with your legs to let her know that running out or stopping before the ditch wasn't an option."

"I'll be sure to apply leg pressure earlier," Julia said, patting Trix's neck. "Good girl."

Callie rode next. She and Jack, often better at dressage, had a good round without hitting any of the jumps. I could see it in Callie's face—she was just relieved that Jack was still sound. She had to be nervous every time he jumped and the fear would probably take a while to fade.

"Go ahead, Sasha," Mr. Conner said.

I took a deep breath, trying to ignore my nerves, and asked Charm to trot. A few strides into the arena, he started to canter.

"Let's do this," I whispered. Charm bobbed his head— he knew we had to work together.

We lined up with the log pile and Charm pricked his ears forward as we approached the logs. He leaped over them, snorting, and cantered to the hay bales. Mr. Conner had three bales side by side in a row and they were all tilted at different angles. I pointed Charm at the middle. He tucked his knees, leaping into the air.

"Good," I whispered. The ditch was strides away, but I wasn't worried. Charm and I had, above all else, trust. He knew I wouldn't let anything hurt him. That's why I was sure he'd get over the ditch the first time.

We reached the ditch and Charm didn't even focus on the tarp. He jumped and landed inches away from the pole on the far side. *Yes!* I cheered in my head. *Okay, okay. Don't lose focus.*

He made it easily over the faux brush and the barrel. Then, gathering himself, he propelled into the air and soared over the picnic table. He landed without touching the table and we cantered back toward the group.

"Perfect," I whispered. "You rock, boy."

Charm flicked his tail. He knew—I didn't have to say it.

We slowed and Charm walked through the exit.

"Wonderful, Sasha," Mr. Conner said. He tapped his clipboard against his leg. "You and Charm continue to shine at cross-country."

"Thanks," I said, beaming.

"Give your horses to Mike and Doug, and I'll see you next time," Mr. Conner said.

Trust, I thought again. Trust was always the key to success in any relationship. With Charm, and with Eric.

32

TRUTH COMES OUT

BY THE TIME CLASSES ENDED, I COULDN'T stand it for another second. I had to fix things with Eric. I owed it to Callie to tell her before I told anyone else about us, so I'd do that. Even if she was upset, there was nothing I could do. I couldn't ruin my relationship with Eric over this.

I checked the time on my phone. I had to meet Jacob in a few minutes to trade film papers at the library. If Callie could meet us there, it would be the perfect chance to tell them both. On my way across campus, I hugged my coat around my body and forced myself to take deep breaths.

Once inside, I snagged an empty table and waited. *You never lied to Callie,* I reminded myself. *You didn't do anything wrong.*

Jacob dropped his book bag on the table with a thud. "Hey," he said, sliding into one of the wooden chairs across from me.

"Hi," I said. "Got your paper?" I wanted to hurry and read each other's papers so I could get the next part over with.

"Sure." Jacob opened his messenger bag and dug through it. Finally, he produced his paper. "You just want to e-mail each other notes later? That way we don't have to sit here and read, I guess," Jacob suggested.

"That's fine."

I took a shaky breath—I had to get this out.

"Jacob," I said. "I need to tell you something."

He put my paper down. "What?" His hazel eyes settled over me.

"I need to talk to Callie too. Do you think you could ask her to meet us here?"

"Okaaay." Jacob stared at me for a second before he texted Callie. A few seconds later, his phone vibrated. "She's on her way."

I nodded. "Thanks."

I looked down and played with the corners of Jacob's paper. I didn't know what else to say. Jacob rocked back on the legs of his chair. We were mostly silent as the minutes ticked by.

"Sasha," Jacob said. "Whatever you have to say—"

"I need to wait for Callie," I said, cutting him off. "Sorry."

Callie, her cheeks flushed from nerves or the cold, walked toward us. She sat by Jacob and across from me—not even bothering to take off her coat.

"What's wrong?" she asked, looking at Jacob and then at me. "Just tell me."

I placed my elbows on the table, resting my chin on my hands. "I don't know how to start, but since you both already know, I'm going to just say it."

I paused. The second I said it, Callie and I could very well be officially over as friends.

"I'm going out with Eric," I said, staring at my hands so I didn't have to see their faces. "I didn't realize that I liked him that way until the last day of the clinic. I should have told you earlier, but I was afraid that you'd think I'd been with him all along—that I'd been lying to you before when I'd said we were just friends. I'm sorry I kept it from you."

I lifted my eyes to look at them. Callie's face was blank—totally unreadable. Jacob just stared at me.

"You're with Eric?" Callie asked in an even tone.

I nodded.

Callie shook her head, seeming confused. "I didn't know that," she said. She looked at Jacob. "Did you?"

"No," he said.

"You didn't?" I asked. "But Jasmine said she'd heard you guys talking about it. She said you told Jacob that if I was dating Eric, our friendship was over."

"I *never* said that," Callie said. "I'm dating Jacob, so why would I be upset if you're with Eric now?"

"I promise I wasn't with Eric until the end of the clinic."

"Sasha, it's okay," Callie said. "I believe you."

I slid back in my chair. Jasmine. Why had I ever believed her? She'd totally had me fooled. She'd known the one thing that would get under my skin, the one big secret I'd been trying to keep, and she'd preyed on it. I couldn't believe that all this—everything getting messed up with Eric at the premiere party—had all been for *what*? To prove she could trick me? To make me feel stupid? *Why*?

I realized Jacob hadn't said a word in a while. He only shuffled through my film paper and occasionally cleared his throat.

"I'm sorry you didn't think you could tell me about Eric," Callie said.

"I was just so afraid of losing you—especially after we'd just gotten our friendship back."

"Of course you were," Callie said. "I was awful to you before when I wouldn't believe that you and Eric were just friends."

Callie and I looked at each other.

"But we can start over," Callie said. "No more secrets?" Callie reached across the table and stuck out her pinky.

I leaned over and linked my pinky to hers. "No more secrets," I echoed.

We smiled, then our eyes shifted over to Jacob. Oops, it had definitely gotten way too emo in here for Jacob— I'd never seen him look so uncomfortable.

He shifted in his seat when both of us looked at him.

"I can go now . . . ," Jacob said.

"I'll go with you," Callie said. She looked at me. "Sasha and I can talk more later, right?"

"Definitely."

While Jacob stuffed his papers into his bag, I walked around the table to stand by Callie.

Callie reached out and hugged me. "I'm happy for you," she whispered in my ear.

As soon as Callie and Jacob left, I shoved Jacob's film paper in my bag. It was time to talk to Eric.

As I walked toward the library's exit, I spotted the Trio across the room. Heather's head was bent over her book. And, as usual, Julia's and Alison's books were closed. Their mouths, however, weren't—they whispered to each other and giggled, soliciting a trademarked librarian's angry "Shhh!"

Courtyard? Pls? I texted Eric.

I walked down and sat on the stone steps. The sun was just starting to set, and shadows crept across campus. Hunching against the cold, I stared at my phone and willed it to beep. While I waited, I rearranged everything in my book bag and twisted my watermelon lip gloss up and down in the tube. *C'mon, Eric,* I thought. *Please text me.* I sighed. He wasn't going to. He was so mad that he—

Buzzzz.

I jumped. "Omigod!" I said to no one.

I flipped open the screen.

Ok.

Yesyesyes!! I ran, skipping the sidewalks and cutting through the grass.

By the time I reached the fountain, I was completely out of breath. Eric stood by the benches, waiting for me. The sun cast a warm orange glow over him. His hands were in the pockets of his brown coat and a piece of hay clung to the hem of his jean leg. He'd been visiting Luna.

"Hi," I said, still breathless.

Eric's eyes locked on mine. "Hey."

I dropped my bag to the ground and stood in front of him. "I'm sorry about Paige's party. I was a jerk, Eric."

"Sash—"

"Please. I need to say this."

Eric nodded.

"I was scared about messing things up for us," I said. "I should have told everyone weeks ago. Even though I was worried about Callie, my relationship with you should have been the most important thing."

Eric didn't move. I watched his face, trying to decide if he was going to walk away or keep listening.

"I really like you, Eric," I said. "I just spoke to Callie and Jacob a minute ago. I told them we're together—and Callie was really happy for us. I'm an idiot for not telling them sooner."

"You're not an idiot," Eric said. "We *both* made mistakes at the party. I should have let you explain. But . . ."

But. Oh, my God. I squeezed my eyes shut. *But* was bad. Always. I'd ruined everything. Again. First Jacob. Now Eric.

Then I felt Eric's strong, warm hand in mine.

"But," he said again, "my biggest mistake was insisting that you still liked Jacob. I'm sorry, Sasha."

"*What*?" I tried to keep my mouth from flopping open. "Are you . . . you're not breaking up with me?"

"Of course I'm not breaking up with you!" Eric said, giving me a soft smile. "Are you kidding? Not a chance."

I threw my arms around him. He smelled *so* good—like mint and clean laundry—and the smell reminded me of the jacket he'd draped over my shoulders after Jacob had dumped me at the Sweetheart Soirée.

Eric held me for a few seconds before stepping back so he could rest his hands on my waist. The fading sunlight lit up his face, and his eyes had that sparkle I loved—and had missed—so much.

"If I broke up with you," he said, "I'd never get to do this again."

He leaned forward and kissed me.

I smiled at him. Eric. My boyfriend. Well, almost. Eric still owed me a date.

33

LIAR

THE NEXT MORNING, PAIGE AND I WERE STILL talking about it.

"It's just *so* romantic," Paige said, putting skinny silver hoops in her ears. "I hope someone kisses me like that someday."

"Of course someone will," I said.

Paige sighed and stared dreamily into her mirror. "But for now, I'll just have to live vicariously through you."

"Fine by me." I giggled.

I smoothed my black wrap sweater and was stepping into my (read: Paige's) ankle boots when my phone buzzed.

Smthng 2 tell u in English.

It was from Callie.

Hint??

She wrote back. *Noo!* ; ⌃) *Wait 4 it.*

:'- (*Mean!*

I put my phone in my pocket. "I can't believe that after everything that's happened, Callie and I are friends *and* I have Eric."

"I'm so happy for you," Paige said. "The secrets are finally over."

"Maybe I can finally get through a day without anything major happening," I said, knocking on my wooden dresser for good measure.

Morning classes dragged on as I waited for English. I'd texted Callie twice to beg her to give me more information, but she'd refused.

When I finally got to English, I felt like I'd downed about thirteen sugar-free energy drinks. I took my seat in Mr. Davidson's classroom and waited for Callie, not even unpacking my books and papers. *Finally,* Callie entered the classroom and hurried over.

"I hate you!" I teased. "You made me wait all day!"

Callie grinned. She dropped her bag on the floor and leaned over to me.

"I shouldn't be smiling 'cause it's scary, but whatever,"

she said. She looked over her shoulder, then back at me. "Jasmine came out of Orchard with the Belles this morning."

"Yeah, so? We knew they were hanging out."

Callie held up a hand. "There's more. They were all laughing, and I distinctly heard Jasmine say, 'They'll be *so* sorry.'"

Uh-oh. "Was she talking about us?"

"Dunno. But she stopped talking when she saw me."

"What if she *was* talking about us—our entire team? Violet, Brianna, and Georgia probably *still* hate us for getting them in trouble."

Callie picked at her chipped chocolate brown nail polish. "But that's so two months ago."

"Yeah, but I've had a couple of fights with Jasmine," I admitted. More than a couple, actually.

We both looked up when Mr. Davidson walked into the room. He went to his desk and picked up his attendance book.

"There's nothing we can do now," Callie whispered. "We'll just have to watch our backs."

We pulled out our phones to finish the conversation.

We can tlk abt it @ riding. I wrote.

Can't come. Got 2 make up quiz 4 math.

Callie and I put away our phones when Mr. Davidson started taking attendance.

So much for one day without drama! Jasmine was probably rallying the Belles against us. The stunt she'd pulled about Callie and Jacob was no small threat. I had to warn the Trio.

After English, Callie and I stepped into the hallway together. "I'm gonna text Heather," I said. "I think we all need to talk."

Callie nodded. "Strange as it sounds to *initiate* talking to her, you're right. Let me know what she says."

"I will."

Callie went left and I went right. I stepped into a side hallway to text Heather.

But when I pulled out my phone, it buzzed before I could type a message.

Movie on Sat? U & me?

Oh, my God. My first official date with Eric!! I forgot all about Jasmine and the Belles and did a nerd dance in the empty hallway.

I tried to type back, but I was so excited that my fingers kept hitting the wrong buttons. I retyped the message twice, then gave up and left it with typos. He'd understand.

Yws! Cab't waut!

It's a date, Eric typed back.

I grinned, hugging my phone to my chest. A date. A REAL date. I needed to get back to Winchester and start online shopping for clothes. Right now.

I saved Eric's message before I put away my phone. Who cared if Jasmine was plotting against us? Maybe she'd been talking about someone else. No more wasting time worrying about something I couldn't control. I'd been doing that for months. If Jas came after the Trio, Callie, or me, we'd handle it. So. There.

Just as I was heading for the exit, one of the classroom doors opened in front of me. Headmistress Drake walked out, her heels clicking sharply against the floor. She stopped in the hallway and turned back to look into the classroom. Her mouth was tight and her arms were folded across her chest.

Julia and Alison walked out, stopping in front of Headmistress Drake. Julia's face was a deep shade of red and she let her short hair fall in front of her eyes. Alison's cheeks were splotchy and her right hand clutched a crumpled tissue, which she used to keep dabbing her eyes. Both of them kept their heads down, not even noticing me, as they shuffled by.

What was going on?

I wanted to say something to them, but the stern look on Headmistress Drake's face told me to stay out of it.

"This way, please," the headmistress said to Julia and Alison, her tone cold and clipped.

She ushered the girls in front of her and they started down the hallway. The students in the hall moved to the side—no one wanted to be in the headmistress's way when she looked that furious. I bet even Georgia—the headmistress's own daughter, apparently—would have moved out of the way.

Julia, Alison, and Headmistress Drake left the building, the door slamming shut behind them. Whispers started the instant the door closed.

"What did they do?" a girl asked.

"I think the blond girl yelled at a teacher," some guy said.

Another girl shook her head, her spiral earrings shaking. "No. Way. Omigod!"

I took out my phone to text Heather. There was no way she already knew about this. I started to type— *OMG, Ju*

I stopped when I saw Jasmine exiting the same classroom Julia, Alison, and Headmistress Drake had just walked out of. I snapped my phone shut and hurried after her.

"What happened?" I asked.

Jasmine stopped and looked at me. She gave me an innocent shrug. "What do you mean?"

"Julia and Alison!" I snapped.

Jasmine smirked. "Oh. That. Like it's a shock, but they cheated on our history exam. They got caught and Mr. Fields called Headmistress Drake."

"They would never do that." But even as I said it, I remembered all the times I'd seen them texting and gossiping rather than studying—even when Heather was doing her work right next to them.

"They wouldn't?" Jasmine asked. "*Please*. They didn't study one bit for this test, and everyone knows it. They thought they could get away with cheat sheets, but Mr. Fields saw them."

I clenched my fingers around my phone. "Did they admit it?"

"Are you stupid?" Jasmine asked, snorting. "Of course they didn't."

"I've gotta go." I left Jasmine standing there and walked away.

"Don't bother running to Princess Heather!" Jas

called after me. "Even she can't save them now."

I pushed the door open and walked outside, glad for the cold air on my warm face. Why would Julia and Alison cheat when they were *this close* to the YENT tryouts? It didn't make any sense. But in my gut, I knew Jas had been right about one thing: Julia and Alison hadn't studied. Even Heather would have to agree.

I started a new text to Heather. *U heard abt Julia & A?*

No. What??

Meet by lib, I typed.

1 min.

I waited at the bottom of the library steps, pacing until Heather arrived.

"What's wrong?" she snapped. Her cashmere scarf had come undone around her neck, and her books were in a messy pile in her arms.

"Julia and Alison just left history class with Headmistress Drake. Jasmine told me that they got caught cheating."

"Oh, God," Heather said. She pressed her fingertips to her lips, shaking her head. "I've got to go." She turned and jogged down the sidewalk.

"Where are you going?" I called after her. But she didn't stop to answer. She was probably headed to the headmistress's office. Not that anyone would let her in, but I knew she wouldn't give up without trying. She cared about Julia and Alison, whether she admitted it or not. She'd do whatever she could to protect them—even when they messed up.

I stood on the steps, unsure what to do. I speed-dialed Callie.

"What's up?" she answered.

"Julia and Alison are in *big* trouble," I said.

"What happened?" Callie asked.

And as I told Callie the whole story, I realized that Julia and Alison were in more trouble than anyone, even Heather, could get them out of.

34

THE VERDICT

I REPLAYED THE SCENE IN MY HEAD FOR THE millionth time. Julia's red face. Alison's teary eyes. The anger in Headmistress Drake's voice.

It had happened just an hour ago, but the entire mood—even in the stable—felt different. I'd wanted to skip my riding lesson, but Callie had talked me into coming. And she was right—we'd just gotten riding privileges back. Not to mention that there was nothing I could do for Julia or Alison if they *had* cheated. Whatever was going to happen, I couldn't stop it. Still, I couldn't help feeling sorry for them.

I remembered how I'd slogged through biology class last fall, often unsure if I'd even pass. My grade had slipped dangerously low, and no matter how much I studied, I kept flunking. It had taken a while before I finally got my grade back up. So I understood how tough it was at Canterwood—the school was known for its superdifficult classes. *But they also didn't study,* I reminded myself.

In the tack room, I grabbed Charm's saddle, pad, and bridle. All of the Trio's tack was still on the racks. Heather *never* missed a lesson.

I pulled open the tack room door and saw Violet on the other side. She stopped what she was doing and stared at me.

"Too bad about Julia and Alison," Violet said, shaking her head. "They'll be lucky to ride again before high school."

I felt the sudden urge to defend them to Violet. "We don't know for sure yet if they really did anything."

Violet laughed and a lock of hair escaped from behind her ear. "Oh, please." She walked toward me, grinning. "Maybe," she said as she passed me, "you'll get your answer in an *e-mail.*"

Ignoring her, I let the tack room door shut, separating us. I had no reason to worry about the Jacob e-mail. I'd already told Callie, so there was nothing Violet could do with it now.

I tacked up Charm and we went to the indoor arena.

He craned his neck to look at me as I slid my foot into the stirrup.

"It's okay, boy," I soothed. "Jack's not going to be here, but you'll see him in the pasture."

I was the only one in the indoor arena. I warmed up Charm for a few minutes, then looked up when hoofbeats echoed in the arena and Heather trotted Aristocrat inside. I definitely didn't expect her to come to the lesson. I examined Heather carefully—she was wearing the same sweater and breeches she'd worn during the last class. And her hair was in a sloppy ponytail under her helmet.

Heather rode Aristocrat up to Charm.

"Did you see them?" I asked.

"They were in the headmistress's lobby," Heather said. "I only had a few seconds to talk to them before Drake's crazy secretary kicked me out."

"And?" I gripped Charm's reins.

Heather shook her head. "They swore they didn't cheat. Julia was practically hysterical. But they sort of calmed down after I said I believed them."

"You really do?" I asked. "After all the times they didn't study?"

"If Julia and Alison tell me that they didn't cheat, then they didn't," Heather said, glaring at me.

Fine. I wasn't going to argue with her. If she believed them, that was fine. But I still wasn't sure. Charm shifted beneath me—he wanted to get away from Aristocrat.

"When do you think we'll know what's going to happen?" I asked.

"Probably after class," Heather said. She started to say something else, but closed her mouth when Mr. Conner walked into the arena. He held up a hand, motioning for us to face him.

"Today, we're going to work on you—the riders," Mr. Conner said, looking at us.

Okay, so he clearly wasn't going to mention Julia's and Alison's noticeable absence. . . . It was weird with just two of us.

"Instead of working the horses, we're going to run through a few stretches and balance exercises for you. As riders, it's important that you're balanced and comfortable in the saddle."

At least this wouldn't require a ton of concentration.

"Spread your horses a few feet apart," Mr. Conner said. "Then we'll get started."

Heather and I separated Aristocrat and Charm.

"Cross your stirrups over the pommel," he said.

We did, and I let my feet dangle against Charm's sides.

"Lean back and grasp the cantle," Mr. Conner instructed. "Hold on and lift your left leg while keeping your knee bent and your heel down."

Heather and I stretched our legs in front of us. My abs tensed and I concentrated on staying centered. Okay, so maybe this wouldn't be as easy as I'd thought.

"Now, bring your leg as far over your horse's neck as you can. But stay centered in the saddle."

I crossed my leg, holding it in the air. I wobbled and tried to keep myself in the saddle. Oww!

"Now, switch legs," Mr. Conner said.

With a grateful sigh, I brought my leg back to its normal position. After Heather and I stretched our opposite legs, Mr. Conner made us do arm circles, twists, and back stretches. By the end of the lesson, Charm was sleepy from standing for forty-five minutes. I, however, was exhausted.

"Great job, girls," Mr. Conner said. "I'll see you tomorrow morning."

We dismounted and led our horses to the crossties. Neither of them needed to be cooled. I untacked Charm, groomed him, and turned him loose in his stall. He nudged my back as I walked to the door.

"I'm sorry," I said. "Forgot your hug."

I squeezed him hard. "I'll give you a special treat tomorrow, okay?"

Charm nodded. I kissed his muzzle and shut the door behind me.

The aisle was deserted—Aristocrat was back in his stall and Heather was already gone.

As I walked back to Winchester, all I could think about was the look on Headmistress Drake's face when she came out of the classroom. One dumb mistake had probably cost Julia and Alison everything. They'd worked so hard to get on the advanced team and to prep for the YENT.

Back in my room, I showered and threw on a pair of worn-soft jeans and an old sweater. Paige was at the library and our room felt too small and quiet. I grabbed my books, Jacob's film paper, and my phone. I left my room and peered into the common room. Empty. Perfect.

I snuggled into the couch and picked up Jacob's film paper. I read the title. *"The Importance of Costume Accuracy in War Films."* Hmm. Did Jacob even like war films?

Just as I was about to start the paper, my phone buzzed and Eric's name popped up on the screen.

"Hey," I said, not able to keep from smiling. Interesting—even amid all of the drama, he still had that effect on me.

"I just heard a rumor that Julia and Alison are in major trouble," Eric said. "True?"

"Yeah, unfortunately. They got caught cheating in history class," I said. "I was right there when Headmistress Drake walked them out."

Eric whistled. "Whoa. That's bad news."

"Totally. *I* was nervous and she wasn't even mad at me."

"What do you think will happen?" Eric asked.

I shrugged, even though he couldn't see me. "I don't know. Heather said—" I looked up and stopped short. "I have to call you back," I murmured, clicking my phone shut. Heather stood in the doorway, her eyes wide and cheeks flushed.

"Heather, what happened?" I asked. But I had a feeling I already knew the answer.

ABOUT THE AUTHOR

Twenty-two-year-old Jessica Burkhart is a writer from New York City. Like Sasha, she's crazy about horses, lip gloss, and all things pink and sparkly. Jess was an equestrian before she started writing and had a horse like Charm. To watch Jess's vlogs and read her blog, visit www.jessicaburkhart.com.

Don't miss what happens next! Pick up the next book
in the CANTERWOOD CREST series:

BEST ENEMIES

October 2009

THE LEADER OF THE TRIO STOOD FROZEN IN
the doorway of the Winchester common room. I never
imagined I'd ever see perfect, fierce Heather Fox like this.
Her face was pale. Her usually glossed lips were bare, and
mascara was smudged beneath her eyes.

My stomach tightened. The news about Julia's and
Alison's fate couldn't be good.

"Heather, what *happened*?" I asked again. "What? Tell
me." I slid off the couch and stood, facing her.

She walked to the fireplace and wrapped her arms
across her chest.

"Heather—" I started.

Her blue eyes were teary when she looked at me. "It's
so awful," she said. "Julia and Alison. They—" Heather

buried her face in her hands and, in that moment, I forgot we were enemies. I just wanted to comfort her.

"C'mon," I said. I put my hand on her elbow and guided her toward the couch. I sat beside her, surprised when she didn't snap at me to get out of her space.

After a few seconds, she sat up straighter and began to talk.

"I waited in Orchard for Julia and Alison," Heather said. "When they finally showed up, they were a mess. They were sobbing and I could barely understand them."

"Okay," I coaxed. "Then what?"

"Julia said that Headmistress Drake called their parents," Heather said. "She told them that Julia and Alison had cheated on their history exam. Alison said they told the headmistress a million times they hadn't, but Headmistress Drake insisted there was proof."

Heather sighed, rubbing her forehead. Whatever she was about to say, I knew it was bad.

Heather took a deep breath, turning to me. Her face was blank. "Julia and Alison got kicked off the advanced team."

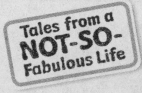

She's a self-proclaimed dork. She has the coolest pen ever. She keeps a top-secret diary.
Read it if you dare.

By Rachel Renee Russell

From Aladdin
Published by Simon & Schuster

City Secrets

Home Sweet Drama

Ruby's Slippers

Nice and Mean

Things Are Gonna Get Ugly

Front Page Face-Off